D1715474

THE
ONTARIO
BEER GUIDE

An Opinionated Guide
to the Beers of Ontario

Jamie MacKinnon

Riverwood

Riverwood Publishers Ltd.
6 Donlands Avenue, P.O. Box 70
Sharon, Ontario L0G 1V0

Canadian Cataloguing in Publication Data

MacKinnon, Jamie
    The Ontario beer guide

Includes bibliographical references.
ISBN 1-895121-15-9

1. Beer – Ontario – Directories.   2. Brewing industry –
Ontario.   3. Breweries – Ontario.   4. Beer – Ontario –
Evaluation.   I Title.

HD9397.C23055   1992   338.7'66342'025713
C92–094844–8

Cover photo by Livingston Photography
Design and typesetting by Heidy Lawrance Associates
Printed and bound in Canada by Webcom

Dedication

with love, for Julie.
Nunc est bibendum.

Table of Contents

FOREWORD: FORWARD!

Are you reading a revolutionary tract?

The author of this book believes that the recent extraordinary changes in beer and brewing—here in Ontario and around the world—are only the start of a long-term revolution in beer. The Ontario beer revolution is a revolt against bland, low- quality beer, and against lousy retailing and lack of choice. It's a revolt against advertising which assumes that you are an idiot.

The Ontario beer revolution is also part of an extraordinary renaissance of beer interest and appreciation now blossoming across the country, in the U.S., Europe and parts of Asia. In Ontario, the revolution was given force by a few brewers who, starting in the mid-1980s, opened shop and dedicated themselves to brewing quality beer. But no commercial or cultural revolution is possible without a public ready to support the aims of the revolt. It's clear that in Ontario, beerdrinkers have been willing and gleeful participants in the beer revolution. Most of us delight in the recent progress and clamour for more.

If the beer revolution now underway in Ontario had a slogan, it would be: "Quality! Variety! No more pap!"

On many an evening, if you listen carefully, you can hear this slogan sung in a certain pub with a revolutionary-military name in downtown Guelph; you can hear it shouted in a tavern on the banks of the Rideau not far from Ottawa, you can hear it over the din in a large and lively bar in the financial district of Toronto. We've heard the slogan in a certain old-style tavern in formerly dry Owen Sound, as well as in a fetching country inn near Madoc.... The beerdrinkers of Ontario, it seems, are determined to see ongoing improvement in the quality and variety of the beer they're offered. The real instigators of the beer revolution are people like you, people who believe that beer is a remarkable and beguiling beverage, one of life's great pleasures.

The major goal of *The Ontario Beer Guide* is to fuel this revolution, to applaud the improvements, and to encourage the changes still needed for Ontario to develop a rich, hardy, and sophisticated beer culture. To do this, the guide aims first to deepen your understanding of and appreciation for beer, particularly the beer brewed in Ontario (chapters one, two, three and four). Second, the guide aims to draw attention to the changes required to further improve the beer scene in Ontario: a better LCBO, a better LLBO, the elimination of anti-competitive beer retailing practices, a better, fairer beer retailing system, better educated servers…the list is long (end of chapter two). Third, by assessing the beer brewed in Ontario, *The Ontario Beer Guide* aims to get a public conversation going, the kind of conversation that provides a context for the improvement of beer, and that educates brewers and beerdrinkers alike (chapter four). Good brewers need educated drinkers as much as educated drinkers need good brewers. Finally, by giving you a chance to participate in a province-wide vote for the best beers brewed in Ontario ("The Beer Ballot" following chapter six), the guide hopes to encourage and expand public interest in a rapidly changing provincial beer scene.

We hope that this first edition of *The Ontario Beer Guide* fulfills some of these aims. If it does, perhaps it is a revolutionary tract. Well, fine. Lovely, placid (not to say complacent) Ontario probably needs the odd incendiary piece of literature.

Cheers!

Jamie MacKinnon
Ottawa, 1992

1
THE GOOD BEER REVOLUTION

The last decade has seen tremendous change in the world of Canadian beer, the greatest change since the end of Prohibition. Most of this change has been for the better—for the industry, for the beerdrinker, for the restaurant and hospitality industry, and for Ontario's beer culture.

After decades of diminishing choice, diminishing flavour, and diminishing numbers of knowledgable beer enthusiasts (is "beer connoisseur" too hoity-toity a term in the democratic world of beer?), things started to turn around in the early 1980s. After decades of "rationalization"—brewery closings, elimination of many lesser-known (but often distinctive) brands, increasing "blandification" and adulteration of the major brands, and concentration of more market share in fewer hands—an abrupt about-turn took place.

New breweries started to spring up, many of them small in capacity, dedicated to brewing high quality, no-short-cuts-taken beer. Brewpubs, illegal until 1985, started to open. Beerdrinkers became more knowledgeable about beer, and more demanding. More of the beer-drinking public started to seek out beer on the basis of quality and variety. Books on beer appeared. Homebrew supply shops opened. And an increasing number of distinctive, flavourful beers came onto the market, brewed right here in Ontario.

All of this amounted to a revolution, a revolt against what had seemed the "inevitable" forces of rationalization and the marketing mentality.

Some of the new beer was darker in colour than the straw-coloured average. Most of it was less carbonated than the highly, and often artificially, carbonated "soda-beer" made by the large breweries. Most of this new beer had noticeable flavour, strong flavour in some cases, the kind of unique and salient flavour that wouldn't—simply *couldn't*—be liked by everyone. It wasn't meant to be. The beer, when drunk, shocked many beerdrinkers who had spent a lifetime drinking something that pretended to be beer: fizzy, flavourless pap, low on barley content and high on advertising.

Not all the beer made by the new breweries was first-rate. But much of it was. And some of it was good enough to fetch the admiration of hard-to-please European beer experts.

It's probably fair to say that the Ontario beer scene is better now than it has been in fifty years. For the drinker, it boils down to having, for the first time in living memory, some *real* variety: bitter, dark ale, stout, continental lager, bock, eisbock, wheat beer. With some curious exceptions—porter, Vienna, brown ale, to name but three—many of the world's great beer styles are now brewed in Ontario.

The beer revolution saw significant change in each Canadian province, but it was in Ontario that change had the greatest effect: the greatest impact on beer variety, on the brewing industry, and on beer appreciation and culture. In Ontario the beer revolution was shaped by our own quirky beer culture, but also affected by similar events elsewhere.

In Britain, a group of thoughtful beerdrinkers who feared the erosion of much of that which best defined excellence in British brewing formed an activist beerdrinkers' group called CAMRA: the Campaign for Real Ale. Since the group's formation in the early 1970s, CAMRA has had a number of successes, and the British beer scene is much the better today for the group's campaigning. Greater beer variety, more "real," cask-conditioned traditional ales, more independent pubs, more brewing competition, and a better educated beerdrinking public are all partly due to CAMRA's work (see glossary for definition of "real ale"). CAMRA has been called the most successful consumer movement in British history.

CAMRA Canada, a spinoff of the British organization, also had some successes pursuing similar goals, including the elimination of barriers to brewpubs.

Another influence which will be referred to again in this book is that of the most famous beer law in the world: the *Reinheitsgebot.* "Reinheitsgebot," according to linguists, is easier to say after drinking one or two good beers. The Reinheitsgebot is a historic and very stringent law which implies the use of yeast and which stipulates that beer be brewed from water, malt, and hops. *Only.* No corn or rice or sugar. No preservatives or "head stabilizers." Just these key ingredients.

The Ontario beer revolution was also influenced by events elsewhere in Canada. In the early 1980s, British Columbia, ahead of the rest of Canada and most of the U.S., witnessed the opening of a few microbreweries (small breweries) and brewpubs (pubs which brew beer on the premises), the first excitement on the national beer scene in quite some time. Following the successes in British Columbia, quality-oriented brewers started to spring up in Washington, Oregon and California, and in Alberta, Ontario, and Quebec. The good beer revolution seemed to snowball as it swept eastward.

Interestingly, even as better quality beers and real variety came to the market, the major national brands —already unexciting, bland and often indistinguishable— got even blander and more alike. Beerdrinkers began to notice that all Big Three beer tasted much the same. Then the Big Three—Molson, Labatt, and Carling-O'Keefe— became the Big Two—Molson and Labatt—who continued to eliminate beers of interest, beers that actually had taste ("marginal" brands, analysts call them), Molson Porter, for example. Was it despite or because of this process of "rationalization" at the large breweries that the beer revolution grew so quickly?

"All the world knows that revolutions never go backward," William Seward once noted, and so it will be with the beer revolution. The beer revolution will continue in the 1990s. Even as you read this, beer attitudes, beer retailing, beer and brewing economics, and beerdrinker demographics are all changing rapidly. More breweries and brewpubs will open in the 1990s (and some will close). You will see more beer appreciation societies, more beer festivals and beer tastings, more beer computer clubs (that's right: some people discuss beer by modem—call it an electronic pub), more and better beer sold in restaurants, as well as increased sophistication among beerdrinkers.

Beer is a remarkable and mysterious...

Beer is a remarkable and mysterious fermented beverage, a complex and nutritious food, the product of the brewer's technique, art, and personality, as well as several thousand years of beer tradition and culture. Consequently, beer is a beverage which doesn't lend itself well to a manufacturing mentality. Beer is not a widget.

In beer, big is often bad. Not because big is inherently bad. But because in Canada, at least, big means that manufacturing and marketing mentalities dominate, and the brewer becomes secondary, a mere technician who maintains consistency and keeps the product rolling off the line.

When brewing becomes just another "profit centre," when the manufacturing mentality permeates the brewery and the bottom line becomes the top concern, beer, the *raison d'être* of the brewing venture, becomes "the product."

The product. We have always been intrigued by the use of this word in large brewing companies, as if beer were a four-letter word. Beer isn't just a manufactured product. Indeed, like any food, beer should never be looked at in this fashion, although this wrong-headed view of beer is common in the large breweries. When beer is seen as a manufactured product, advertising, marketing, and "product positioning" are seen as the main link between the brewery and the drinking public, not the beer.

With a view of beer as "product," the manufacturing mentality keeps looking for ways to use cheaper or fewer hops, to use less costly barleymalt and more cheap adjunct (like corn syrup), to reduce conditioning time, to cut transportation costs—the list is long. Then, when the product is uniform, bland and cheap, the manufacturing mentality asks the marketing mentality to devise a pretty package and to flog, flog, flog the product.

The end result of this approach to brewing, this process of "rationalization," is a peculiar, late-twentieth-century form of idiocy: it is you watching TV, staring in bafflement at some steely-eyed, slack-jawed young man who is ogling a young, vacantly smiling, bikini-clad woman who has entered the picture by (how else?) parachute. And you end up wondering about the connection between the advertisement and beer.

Most of the idiotic beer ads on TV have little to do with beer. Many of the boys (we can't help using this term) at the big breweries appear to believe that beer has more to do with sexual insecurity, peer group pressure, psychological image, and fancy packaging than with ingredients, style and quality. *The Ontario Beer Guide* is based on the premise that this view of beer is dead wrong, and underestimates the beerdrinking public.

The idiocy of TV beer ads is only one manifestation of the lack of reason in "rationalization" and the beer-as-widget approach to beer. Serious beerdrinkers also point to the irrationality of a process which presumes that everyone wants to drink the same, middle-of-the-road suds sold under different labels. Thoughtful beerdrinkers see irrationality (and contempt) in an attitude which presumes that no one notices as corn and other cheap adjuncts increasingly replace barley malt—the key reason the national brands became "national blands" in the 1960s, 70s and 80s.

Many thoughtful, nationalistic beerdrinkers and industry analysts have also pointed to the faulty reasoning of this blandification process when the result is increased similarity to bland, mainstream, American beer. These drinkers and analysts point to the long-term cost of gradually losing the attribute that has traditionally maintained Canadian beerdrinkers' loyalty to mainstream Canadian beer: detectable malt and hop flavour. Reason tells us that when mainstream Canadian beer tastes the same as mainstream American beer, beerdrinkers will quickly learn to shop solely on the basis of price.

Perhaps blandification has its own reasoning, or rationalization. But it is the reasoning of someone who has forgotten, or never known, that beer is a remarkable and mysterious fermented beverage. Beer, the "ancientest and wholesomest drink," comes in an astonishing variety of styles and sub-styles: dark, chocolaty stouts; bitters, sometimes highly bitter and grainy, sometimes lightly bittered and rounded; porters with hints of burnt grain and espresso; fruit beers (raspberry, cherry, peach, etc.); dry, crisp pilsners; malty, semi-sweet Viennas; complex and seductive brown ales; tart, lemony wheat beers— these are but a few of the world's beer styles. Even more than wine, there's a beer for every season, for every occasion, for every palate.

Beer is simple. Anyone can make it. Its essential ingredient is barley malt. Boil the malt, add hops, pitch yeast, and *voilà*. Beer is extraordinarily complex, like music, food, and literature. Show any interest in it, and you discover that you can deepen your beer knowledge and appreciation over a lifetime.

Beer (sharing the spotlight with bread) is one of the greatest achievements in the history of domestic science and food preparation: the transformation of barley grain into a foam-covered glass of lightly carbonated beer is alchemy indeed!

Beer is a balm to the spirit and food for the soul. Beer is an extraordinary and seductive potion.

In essence, this is what the good beer revolution is about: an understanding of what beer is at its best, what it has been in its millenniums-old history, and what it can be in the years ahead. The good beer revolution is a revolt against beer as "product" and an insistence that beer should always be a remarkable, mysterious, and beguiling beverage.

2
ONTARIO'S BEER CULTURE AND BEER SCENE

"They who drink beer will think beer."
—Washington Irving, *The Sketch Book*

While Canada is an important beer nation in some regards—
in terms of production, exports, and per capita consumption, it
is among the top twenty beer countries in the world—it lacks
something without which it cannot be a great beer nation. It
lacks a sophisticated beer culture.

Belgium, Britain, Ireland, Germany, Denmark and
Czechoslovakia take beer seriously. Not too seriously, mind
you, not solemnly, but with the respect and interest that
this ancient and admirable drink deserves. Beerdrinkers in
these countries understand beer to be something carefully
chosen, properly served, contemplatively considered, and
drunk with pleasure.

What is a beer culture? Where people drink and think
about beer, where people talk and read about beer, a beer
culture evolves. A beer culture connotes a knowledgeable
public, committed and exacting brewers, good pubs and
beer-wise restaurants, public beer events (often tied to the
rhythms of the beer calendar), and words—magazines and
books, beer journalism in newspapers, beer-tasting seminars,
pub talk, and so on. In other words, a beer culture needs
beer knowledge and beer conversation.

In Ontario some of these elements are falling into place,
but we still have a distance to go. Too many people and too
much beer advertising still assumes that beerdrinkers are
uneducated boobs: they drink, but they don't think. Too

often, when we enter a quality bookstore and ask for books or magazines on beer we get a look of incomprehension or condescension. Ask for a book or a magazine on wine, and we often get a different response. Too often, we cannot get a choice of quality beers at otherwise good restaurants. Too often when we ask questions about beer sold at a Liquor Control Board of Ontario (LCBO) store, employees can't provide the answers.

To develop a better beer culture in Ontario, we need progress on several fronts. We need more knowledgeable publicans and servers. We need restaurateurs who understand that an excellent beer can complement a meal every bit as well as (and sometimes better than) wine. We need more stringent rules that require pubs to have a minimum number of competing brands of draught beer available.

We need more media discussion of *beer*—not price increases, or new advertising campaigns, or beer-related trade negotiations, which the media tend to cover fairly well— but beer itself: new beer brands, beer ingredients, beer style, beer tastings, good places to drink, etc.

We need beer advertising that is less sexist and less stupid. We need advertising that provides information on key beer concerns such as price, ingredients and beer style. The large breweries can, but seldom do, address these concerns in their advertisements, though it must be acknowledged that some silly regulations govern beer advertising. The Liquor Licence Board of Ontario (LLBO), for example, constrains brewers from giving any precise price information to the public. The Canadian Radio-Television Commission (CRTC) prohibits advertisements that show beer being drunk!

We need national laws that require brewers to put ingredients on the label or carton. The European Community is moving toward such laws.

Ontario needs minimum standards of beer knowledge for those who retail beer. Beerdrinking Ontarians need a Ministry of Consumer and Commercial Relations that takes the interests of beer consumers as seriously as the interests of the large breweries. Ontario needs a much more customer-driven LCBO.

Finally, what Ontario really needs to develop a strong and sophisticated beer culture is a change in attitude, outlook and procedure at our large breweries and in "The Beer Store." We will look at how the large brewers and the retail system inhibit the growth of a sophisticated beer culture later. But first, let's look briefly at Ontario's beer heritage and various aspects of the Ontario beer scene today.

Ontario's beer roots

Beer has its own culture, a culture that varies with time and place. Ontario's beer culture and traditions faintly echo their European roots, and have been heavily influenced by both our pioneer history and by patterns of immigration.

Canadian brewing got its start in New France in the seventeenth century. In 1666 Intendant Jean Talon asked permission from the French colonial powers to build a brewery for the growing number of settlers in the St. Lawrence river valley. He received this reply:

> If the use of beer is introduced for good in Canada, and the people get used to it, as they should, for this beverage is good and healthy in itself...The money will remain in the country and drunkenness and the vices which generally accompany it shall no longer be the cause of scandal, by reason of the cold nature of beer, the vapours whereof rarely deprive men of the use of judgment.

Commercially produced beer thus got started, and by the 1670s the Brasserie du Roy in Quebec City was brewing to such a capacity it could export to the West Indies.

As settlers moved westward, they brought their brewing knowledge, techniques and preferences with them. Ontario's earliest European settlers—the French, the Scots, the English and then the Irish—all brought with them beer preferences. These preferences were constrained by the availability and cost of barley and hops, by local soils and the strains of barley and hops they would support, and also by temperature and season. (Later, ice cut from lakes would have a role to play in beer storage). And of course, the brewing capabilities, knowledge and lore of the early brewers greatly affected what they were able to offer.

It appears to us that the nineteenth century pioneers of Ontario have had two quite different influences on beer and brewing in Ontario. On the one hand, the pioneers were characterized by self-reliance, sound commercial instincts, and the idea that a pint or two of decent beer was a man's (and to a lesser extent a woman's) mete reward at the end of a hard day. Spruce beer, still brewed on occasion by home-brewers, was often brewed by pioneers in Canada, and is Canada's unique contribution to the family of specialty beers. Imagine a beer designed to fight scurvy! Many of our pioneer ancestors saw beer as a moderate, pleasurable drink. They saw it as a reminder of social life in the countries they'd left, and they were happy to imbibe a few pints at their local tavern or inn.

On the other hand, some of the pioneers had a strong puritan streak, which saw alcohol as a Bad Thing. The result was the temperance movement, some ridiculous beer laws, and Prohibition. "Temperance" societies were so numerous in the 1870s that they formed a federation, the Dominion Alliance for the Total Suppression of the Liquor Traffic. The Woman's Christian Temperance Union urged drinkers to "take the pledge" to stop drinking alcohol. "Pledge cards" from the WCTU were used in the fight against alcohol. One such pledge card employs the almost-Biblical injunction "Touch Not, Taste Not, Handle Not."

Official prohibition came to Ontario in 1927, but enjoyed less than total support. "I wish somehow we could prohibit the use of alcohol," said Stephen Leacock in reaction to the anti-alcohol brigade, "and merely drink beer and whiskey and gin as we used to."

The puritanical streak ridiculed by Leacock has persisted even to the present in Ontario as an influence on beer, especially on how beer is sold, and where, when and even how it is drunk. Are you old enough to remember not being allowed to drink standing up in an Ontario bar? Can you remember the Brown Paper Bag laws? Being required to write your name and address to buy alcohol at the LCBO? While alcohol puritanism diminished considerably in the 1960s and 70s, Ontario is still, in comparison with most of North and South America and Europe, very highly regulated with respect to alcohol.

Commercial brewing got rolling in the early 1800s in Upper Canada. Ian Bowering covers a good deal of Ontario's early brewing history in his excellent book, *The Art and Mystery of Brewing in Ontario*. Bowering tells us that the most important influence in the 19th century was the British military presence. Military men expected and received ale as part of their rations. Four to six pints a day was the norm at one time!

Because so many of the first non-native settlers in Ontario were of British extraction, British beer attitudes and brewing knowledge have had a very major influence on our beer culture, especially on the beer styles that have been brewed. British ale styles—pale ale and bitter, porter, stout, and brown ale—were the most commonly produced commercial beers right up to the end of the nineteenth century when lager started to gain hold. Porter, stout and brown ale diminished in popularity between the wars, but local variations of the "pale ale/bitter" style remained the beer of choice for most Ontarians. In Ontario, Quebec and Atlantic Canada, these variations gradually evolved into a beer style that Canada can claim as its own: Canadian ale. (See "Beer Styles of Ontario" for further information on style characteristics.)

The "Canadian ale" style of beer is an important facet of Ontario's beer heritage. Derived from the pale ale/bitter style of Britain, it is (or was) characterized by a grainy-husky flavour imparted by the use of Canadian six-row barley, as opposed to the rounded, sometimes soft, sometimes fruity character of British pale ale styles that use two-row barley. In the 1960s, Export, Black Horse, Red Cap and Stock Ale typified the Canadian ale style as we define it, but the style has lost much of its character, and perhaps even disappeared, due in large part to the increasing proportion of adjunct and the decreasing levels of hop bitterness at the large breweries. To a lesser extent, the disappearance of the Canadian ale style is due to increasing use of two-row barley.

While the conventional dictionary definition of lager emphasizes "bottom fermentation" and the yeasts that enable it, lager is really a low-temperature approach to beer. Lager became a viable alternative in Ontario just after Confederation, when better technical and temperature control made low-temperature fermentation an option for the brewer. Growing numbers of German immigrants also meant a growing market for lager.

Other influences on beer and brewing in Ontario in this century are worldwide phenomena: increasing pasteurization and artificial carbonation of beer, a century-long shift away from casks or kegs to bottles and lately, cans, and growing use of low-cost adjunct (like corn and rice) as beer ingredients. Opposed to these global forces have been more recent trends in Ontario: beer appreciation societies, the homebrewing movement, "walk-in breweries," microbreweries and brewpubs, and bars which offer an increasingly broad selection of local, quality beers.

Ontario has traditionally been divided on its ale and lager consumption patterns, a tradition which is less true today, with the ascendancy of lager, but which still holds to a large extent. Eastern and Northern Ontario have been ale strongholds, while Southwestern Ontario, influenced in part by German settlers in the Kitchener area, drinks more lager than the east and the north. To an extent, ale is consumed in Catholic Ontario; lager in Protestant Ontario.

One used to hear this pattern simplified: east of Yonge Street, ale; west of Yonge Street, lager. Of course, it was never this simple; lots of ale gets drunk in southwestern Ontario, and the folks in Eastern Ontario have quaffed more than a few steins of lager.

The most recent significant influence on the Ontario beer scene is immigration, and the effect that newcomers' beer preferences have on the beer market. Upper Canada's Sichuan Waves beer was introduced at least in part to cater to Oriental restaurants and to East Asian beerdrinkers' preference for light-bodied beer made with rice as an adjunct. Banks beer was introduced at least in part to appeal to Ontarians of Caribbean ancestry.

Ontario's beer culture is the product of all these influences. While large breweries dominated the beer scene in Ontario from the 1930s to the 1970s, it's important to remember that, taking the long view, this was an aberration. Earlier times in Ontario were marked by a multitude of local brewers serving local markets.

In the nineteenth century, towns as small as Tecumseh, Georgetown, Goderich, Trenton, New Hamburg, and Kemptville had breweries to serve local folks and farmers in the hinterland. Few people lived far from a brewer. This had the advantage of providing local employment and a market for local barley and in some places, local hops. It also meant that most beer was fresh and served on tap. At the time of Confederation, Ontario had more than 100 independent brewers.

Now, with a beer renaissance well under way, Ontario is really returning to its roots. More and more cities, towns and even villages are getting their own breweries and brewpubs. It seems increasingly possible that we may once again see 100 brewers in Ontario!

Now, like earlier times, many Ontario beerdrinkers have a tantalizing "local option." Now, more than at any time in the past fifty years, Ontario beerdrinkers also have real variety available to them from the growing number of Ontario

brewers. These happy facts make us think that a sophisticated and vital Ontario beer culture will start to take root
and develop in the years ahead.

The beer scene in Ontario

Ontario is *the* beer province in Canada. It consumes the
most beer and it has the greatest number of breweries. The
figures below show a general trend of declining beer consumption, although they do not reflect the great growth in
homebrewed beer during the 1980s. Against this background, the figures show that Ontario recently edged past
the biggest per capita beer drinkers of 1980, Quebec and
Newfoundland, to become the greatest beer-imbibing
province in the Dominion, on a per capita basis.

Per capita consumption of beer (in litres)

	1990	1980
Ontario	83.36	88.19
Newfoundland	82.19	88.88
British Columbia	80.39	76.26
Quebec	80.33	92.16
Alberta	70.45	67.20
Nova Scotia	68.13	75.09
Manitoba	66.51	79.36
New Brunswick	64.54	78.55
P.E.I.	64.22	74.81
Saskatchewan	55.13	74.61
Canada	**78.16**	**84.31**

International figures for comparison (1989)

(West) Germany	144
Czechoslovakia	131.8
Denmark	123.4
Belgium	114.9
U.K.	110.4
U.S.	89.0

source: Brewers Association of Canada

It's interesting to consider that four of the five provinces which consume the most beer—Ontario, B.C., Quebec, and Alberta—are also home to almost all the country's micro-breweries. Consequently, these four provinces offer the greatest beer variety to the beerdrinking public. Do people in P.E.I. (which has no in-province brewery) and Saskatchewan (which brews almost exclusively the pale, bland, "international style" lager) drink relatively little beer because they can't get a wide variety of good local beers?

Likewise, it's interesting to consider the parallel situation suggested by the international figures. Five of the countries that drink significantly more beer per capita than does Canada—Germany, Czechoslovakia, Denmark, Belgium, and Britain—happen to be countries that take beer and beer culture seriously, and that brew some of the world's best beer.

Ontario is not only the biggest beerdrinking province in Canada, it is also the biggest brewing province in terms of the number of breweries and brands it supports. Ontario has more than a dozen breweries—roughly twice as many on a per capita basis as the United States. (Belgium, with almost the same population as Ontario, has roughly eight times as many breweries!) Including the beers brewed in its 30-odd brewpubs, Ontario has about 140 different brands of beer.

Ontario, after decades of diminishing beer choice and a withering beer culture, shows signs of a real beer renaissance. This is true in other parts of Canada as well, but Ontario, at least in terms of beer variety, has become the beer and brewing capital of Canada. Should we advertise this fact on roadsigns at Ontario's borders? Perhaps the idea is not that silly. Other countries understand the contribution a beer culture can make to society and the economy.

Look at Germany. Over 20 million tourists visit Germany each year, 300,000 of them from Canada. In a 1987 survey, "the tourist board found that German beer was the most important reason for choosing West Germany as a vacation spot...followed by castles and cathedrals, landscape and nature, German villages and German wine" (*The Globe and Mail*). Ontario's burgeoning beer scene would seem to bode well for marketing the province to beer-interested tourists.

Is it all good news on the beer front in Ontario? Here, and in the U.S. and Britain, many beerdrinkers and beer analysts have been concerned about the continuing decline of ale as a portion of all beer drunk.

The following table illustrates the ailing of ale in the 1980s.

The death of ale?
Percentage of beer sold in Canada by type

	Ale		Lager		Light	
	1988	1978	1988	1978	1988	1978
Newfoundland	6.9	34.8	86.7	65.2	6.4	0.0
New Brunswick	10.1	24.4	79.1	75.6	10.8	0.0
Nova Scotia	59.5	71.3	32.8	28.7	7.7	0.0
P.E.I.	18.2	30.4	71.4	69.6	10.5	0.0
Quebec	71.5	94.8	23.0	5.2	5.6	0.0
Ontario	21.8	50.4	60.7	49.6	17.5	0.0
Manitoba	0.7	3.1	72.9	96.9	26.4	0.0
Saskatchewan	0.0	2.0	72.7	98.0	27.3	0.0
Alberta	0.2	3.5	82.4	96.5	17.5	0.0
B.C.	0.7	2.5	92.6	97.5	6.7	0.0
Canada	**30.1**	**53.4**	**56.8**	**46.6**	**13.1**	**0.0**

source: Brewers Association of Canada

The trends in Ontario and Canada reflect a long-term, world-wide pattern: the "lagerization" of the world. The decline of ale in traditional ale-drinking countries (Britain, Ireland, Canada, the U.S., and perhaps New Zealand and Australia) to the benefit of lager is a century-old trend. In the late 1800s, improvements in refrigeration and the cultivation of bottom-fermenting yeasts made production of lager (until then brewed widely only in parts of Germany) more feasible for more brewers. The decline of ale to the benefit of "light" is a more recent trend, and reflects changing demographics, especially the aging of the baby boom, and an increasingly calorie-conscious population.

In 1978, half the beer drunk in Canada—and Ontario —was ale, making Canadian beerdrinkers quite unlike their American counterparts. In the U.S., the trend away from ale to greater lager consumption started earlier, and lager has long taken a much larger share of the U.S. beer market than it has in central and eastern Canada. By 1988, however, less than one beer in three drunk in Canada was ale, and ale still continues to decline.

In recent history, only two provinces in Canada have drunk more ale than lager—Nova Scotia and Quebec—but the trend to lager persists even in these two ale-drinking provinces. Ontario beerdrinkers drank more ale than lager until 1979. The western provinces, which may best be termed La-lager Land, have drunk lager almost exclusively in recent history. The three largest light-drinking provinces, Manitoba, Saskatchewan and Alberta, are also provinces where ale is ailing (or in Saskatchewan's case, dead). One might have thought that the flat, featureless prairie would make one want to avoid flat, featureless beers, but this is apparently not the case.

Note the beer blight in Saskatchewan. In 1988 Saskatchewan registered no sales of ale whatsoever—no pale ale, brown ale, porter or stout—according to the Brewers Association of Canada statistics. Things have improved of late in Canada's un-beer province, with the opening of several brewpubs, but ale-lovers may still want to take their holidays elsewhere.

Canada's two greatest (if that is not too strong a word) stout and porter drinking provinces were Quebec and Ontario where together these two beer styles claimed two bottles per thousand (0.2%) of the provincial beer markets, roughly half of their marketshare a decade ago. With new microbrewery stouts recently introduced in these two provinces, perhaps dark ales will find a growing market.

The statistical tables above and below reveal a problem of another type. "Light" is not a beer style. "Light" doesn't even tell us if the beer is top-or bottom-fermented (ale or lager). The "light" category reduces the value of the statistics because light isn't a style. Are Wellington County's Arkell Best Bitter and S.P.A., with 4 and 4.5% alcohol-by-volume respectively, "light" beers, in the same category as Molson Light and Labatt's Blue Light? Should we classify a full-flavoured, 3.9% alc./vol. brown ale as a "light" beer? No serious beerdrinker could entertain the thought.

The following table details the trends to lager and "light" in Ontario over a five-year period.

Percentage of beer sold in Ontario by type

	Ale	Lager	Light	Malt liquors, stouts & porters
1987	23.3%	61.0%	15.1%	0.6%
1988	22.3%	60.7%	16.3%	0.7%
1989	21.1%	60.7%	16.3%	0.6%
1990	19.5%	63.1%	16.9%	0.5%
1991	18.7%	63.5%	17.3%	0.5%

source: Brewers of Ontario

What does lagerization mean for the beerdrinker? Is it all bad news? We think the answer is: maybe. It just depends.

We like lager. Well-hopped pilsners and Dortmunders are wonderful beer styles, fascinating members of the beer family. Bocks and Viennas are complex and intriguing examples of darker lagers. Unfortunately, most of the lager making up the lagerization trend is insipid, "international-style" lager. Even lager fans, that is, fans of flavourful and interesting lager styles, won't cheer this trend. And we

believe that lager fans have cause for concern in the continuing decline of ale. Quite simply, in a country like Canada,
where the variety of beer styles and flavours is already quite
limited, the continuing decrease of sales within a major beer
style bodes poorly for variety in the future.

On the other hand, while the gain of lager at the
expense of ale is a significant, worldwide, century-old trend,
no trend lasts forever. Ale is a large group of diverse beer
styles, with much to offer the beerdrinker. Ale already
shows signs of regaining popularity in parts of the U.S. and
Europe.

In the near term, however, lagerization will continue in
Ontario. This is partly due to the fact that most of the very
cheapest product sold at the LCBO is classified as "lager,"
though we think this too generous a word for the bland,
canned beverage that forms the greatest part of the LCBO's
beer sales. As trade in beer opens up, low-end (mostly
American, mostly canned) lager will gain a greater share of
the Ontario beer market.

Let's look at a ten-year snapshot of beer sales at the
LCBO:

Beer sales at the LCBO

	Domestic		Imported	
	'80-81	'90-91	'80-81	'90-91
Sales in litres	37,468,000	43,242,000	4,855,000	33,382,000
Sales in dollars	$42,148,000	$114,483,000	$11,991,000	$90,882,000
Ten-year increase in domestic beer sales by volume:			+ 15.4%	
Ten-year increase in domestic beer sales by value:			+ 172%	
Ten-year increase in imported beer sales by volume:			+ 586%	
Ten-year increase in imported beer sales by value:			+ 658%	

source: LCBO

These figures reflect a trend that will likely continue and
perhaps accelerate: the gain of imported beer at the expense
of domestic. While the total sale of domestic beer at the

LCBO and at Brewers Retail increased only marginally during the 1980s (up 15.4% by volume), sales of imports skyrocketed.

Of greater concern to the major domestic brewers is that this loss of marketshare should occur in a retail system which has been stacked against foreign brewers who would like to compete. When Ontario removes some of its discriminatory trade barriers, as it is and will be doing, the major brewers will see their share of the Ontario market erode even more rapidly. Imports now have less than 5% of the Ontario market. We believe that within a few years, imports will grab 10-20% of the market.

This significant shift is unlikely to affect the viability of small, quality-oriented breweries in Ontario, who now have 5-6% of the market. Microbreweries continue to build marketshare in Ontario (but at a slower rate than in previous years), so it is really the large breweries who are suffering and who will suffer the most from increased beerdrinker interest in imports.

Ironically, increased import sales, which in theory should be good news for beerdrinkers who care about variety, may in the case of Ontario be bad news for the future of variety and quality.

Why bad news? The imports that are making waves in the market are not high quality beers from Britain, Belgium or Germany, but the famous Wet Air products sold so cheaply south of the border.

Rank of imported beers at the LCBO (1989-90)

(previous year's rank in brackets)

1.	Old Milwaukee	(1)	6.	Schlitz	(20)
2.	Heileman Lone Star	(4)	7.	Heineken	(2)
3.	Miller's Milwaukee Best	(12)	8.	Corona Extra	(3)
4.	Old Milwaukee Light	(16)	9.	Beck's	(7)
5.	Miller's Meistbrau	(5)	10.	Michelob	(9)

Sales for Beck's and Heineken—the only two quality beers on the list, in our opinion—declined from the previous year. Note that not a single ale is to found on the list. Overall then, most of the import pattern and the changes from the previous year can be explained by the large number of beer-drinkers for whom cost—not quality—is the sole consideration. The top American sellers are all cheap product: not a flavourful, Reinheitsgebot beer among them. Some of the cheapest American "beer" has less barley malt in it than adjunct.

Molson and Labatt are therefore faced with a serious dilemma. They will have a good deal of trouble competing on a cost basis with the large U.S. breweries. But by making their own beers more bland and adjunct-laden year after year, the Big Two brewers have created a growing market for Wet Air. And the Americans, who have perfected the art of making Wet Air cheaply, will be only too happy to satisfy that market.

We believe that the most viable future for Labatt and Molson, essentially second-tier breweries on a world basis in terms of size, is to dedicate themselves to mid-to-high quality, higher-value-added, higher cost beers. So far, we don't see this happening. Will the sleeping execs at Molson and Labatt rouse themselves in time?

A brewpub revolution?

A significant aspect of the ongoing beer revolution and Ontario's changing beer scene is the recent legalization and extraordinary proliferation of brewpubs.

A brewpub is simply a pub that has a small brewery on the premises. Unlike non-brewpub breweries, brewpubs cannot sell their beer off-premises. This limits the amount of beer brewpubs can sell, but it also eliminates the need for (and the high cost of) a bottling system and a distribution network. It also means that the (draught) beer they sell can be very fresh, as draught beer should be.

In Ontario, brewpubs have been legally limited to an

annual production of 2,000 hectolitres per year (one hectolitre = 100 litres), although there is pressure to increase
this limit.

The number of brewpubs in Ontario has grown phenom-
enally since they were first legalized in 1986. By 1989 or
1990, there were more brewpubs than breweries, and eventually, there are likely to be *many* more brewpubs than
breweries. This guide lists more than two dozen brewpubs,
and there will be more on the scene by the time you read
this. If we treat brewpubs as breweries, Ontario will have
about 60 "breweries" (breweries proper, plus brewpubs) by
the mid-1990s. And to think: not long ago, beer analysts
were predicting that Ontario would soon have only one or
two breweries!

Estimated production of selected Ontario brewpubs

	Hectolitres per annum (1990)
Amsterdam Brasserie (Toronto)	1500
Denison's Brewing/Growler's Restaurant (Toronto)	1250
Rotterdam Brewing (Toronto)	1000
The Lion Brewery & Museum (Waterloo)	1000
Marconi's Steak and Pasta House (Etobicoke)	660
The Master's Brasserie & Brewpub (Ottawa)	600

source: All About Beer, Oct.-Nov. '91

A hectolitre is the equivalent of just over twelve 24-bottle
cases of beer. According to a brewpub survey conducted by
the Institute for Brewing Studies, brewpubs tend to sell
twice as much of their own beer as bottled and "guest"
draught beers. If this is true, then brewpubs would appear to
be very lucrative, at least potentially. When a single brewpub can sell a thousand hectolitres—100,000 litres—of its
own brewed-on-premises beer, and not have to worry about
beer transportation, bottle returns, or a beer strike, you can
be certain that more and more business people will take an

interest. (Some of them will open great new brewpubs; some of them, motivated only by profit, will open mediocre brewpubs.)

From a beer-quality point of view, the brewpubs in Ontario are generally of two orders: the very good, and the mediocre or poor. Poor and mediocre brewpubs tend to suffer from a lack of management commitment to quality beer, from an indifference to style, from a lack of interest in brewing seasonal and specialty beers, and from less than fanatical attention to cleanliness. Some brewpubs also suffer from taking the brewpub shortcut: brewing not from barley malt, but from malt extract, a syrup made from barley malt. It's possible to make good brewpub beer from malt extract, but great brewpub beer is most often brewed from barley malt. Brewing from barley malt is commonly called "all mash" or "brewed from grain" brewing.

Given the successful growth of brewpubs to date in Ontario, and the fact that cities can support more than one—Metro Toronto has roughly a dozen—we predict many more brewpubs in years to come. As brewpubs become more common and beerdrinkers more demanding, we will also see some of the poorly run brewpubs go out of business.

It is becoming common wisdom in the brewpub business that, in order to succeed, a brewpub must consistently provide first-class beer *and* first-class food. Ontario's best brewpubs are great places to eat. More and more Ontarians are discovering the epicurean pleasures of a good meal accompanied by fresh beer (or vice versa, depending on your point of view) at their local brewpubs. Brewpubs also need well-trained, beer-knowledgeable staff.

Good beer, good food, good service: quality-oriented brewpubs provide them all.

Impediments to the growth of a sophisticated Ontario beer culture: Brewers Retail, the LCBO, and the big brewers

While Ontario has seen a good deal of progress for the beer-drinker in the past ten to fifteen years, some serious barriers to progress—call them hurdles on the path to beerdrinkers' heaven—remain. These barriers will be overcome, but don't hold your breath. Have a good beer instead.

Many of the most serious problems—from a consumer's point of view—can be blamed on Brewers Retail, the LCBO, and some attitudes and practices at the large breweries. Also to blame for many of the beer-related problems detailed below are the three main political parties who, when it comes to beer, tend to support the status quo at the expense of fairness, the ecology, and the consumer.

In many ways, beer retailing in Ontario exhibits the worst aspects of oligopolistic big business on the one hand and state control on the other. An honest brew should be able to make its own friends, but unfortunately our monopoly retailing system makes it very difficult for some honest brews to find their way to market. Consider how the Brewers Retail-LCBO monopoly looks to an outsider, someone used to knowledgeable and courteous service when buying beer. To someone used to walking (!) to the nearest convenience store to buy beer, or even (brace yourself) buying local beer, imported beer, wine, groceries and newspapers in the *same* (!) store.

One European-born beer connoisseur who has had some experience trying to deal with Brewers Retail and the LCBO once told us that an antipathy to and an ignorance about beer seemed to be the sole criteria for getting a job at either establishment. "Why," he asked with astonishment, "do Ontarians put up with such rotten service?" It's a question well worth asking.

Brewers Retail

Brewers Retail Incorporated, nominally a "co-operative," is a *privately owned retail monopoly,* the only such monopoly in the world. Few Ontarians know this, perhaps because our media, who take so many advertising dollars from Brewers Retail's owners, seldom write critically about it.

Brewers Retail, alias "The Beer Store," is almost entirely owned by Molson and Labatt (Northern Breweries owns a very small portion, about 1%, as does Amstel). This "co-operative" acts very much like a private company, in large part doing the bidding of its majority owners. Brewers Retail can refuse to sell equity to smaller breweries, and thus deny them the chance to influence policy.

The LCBO is not a viable alternative for small brewers: LCBO policy restricts beer sales to one brand per domestic brewery, and the LCBO tends to retail poorly the beer they do sell (see below). Small brewers must therefore rely on Brewers Retail, a retail monopoly owned by their largest competitors! For this reason alone, if alcohol were not a jealously guarded provincial jurisdiction, the Bureau of Competition Policy in Ottawa would almost certainly demand significant changes in Ontario's beer retailing system.

As the major shareholders of the company, Labatt and Molson can largely determine how, when and even whether small Ontario breweries sell their beer (and how, when and even whether consumers can buy it). If Brewers Retail wants to shut the whole retail system down, it apparently can. In 1985, you may remember, a lockout at one of the major breweries led to the closing down of the entire Brewers Retail network. Although the lockout was often reported as a strike, it was in fact a lockout, a management tactic in a contract dispute. Had this been a simple management-labour conflict, the consequence would have been local and unimportant. The brewery involved would have used management to run the plant, or accepted the fact that beer couldn't be brewed until the dispute was settled.

However, because the company involved also had a controlling position in Brewers Retail, the results were much more unjust and costly to the Ontario public. The doors of Brewers Retail were locked, and small breweries were shut out of their major retail outlet. Consumers could not buy beer at Brewers Retail from breweries unaffected by the labour dispute. That is to say, a retail monopoly controlled by the two largest brewers severely constrained the market access of several small brewers. The cost to the Ontario economy was estimated by analysts to be in the tens of millions of dollars, a cost largely borne by waiters, waitresses, and publicans.

Many beerdrinkers were shocked to find out that this kind of action—contrary to many tenets of common law, and contrary to a sense of fair play—was possible. Many beerdrinkers were shocked to discover that in Ontario, most beer retailing is done at the pleasure of the two largest breweries. In the aftermath of this arrogant slap in the face of the province's beerdrinkers, Brewers Retail became a little more circumspect. The appearance was that this retail monopoly would not further antagonize the beer-drinking public, at least until the 1985 lockout faded from memory. But as far as we can determine, nothing has changed to prevent another costly shutdown from occurring whenever it suits Brewers Retail's owners, although ongoing trade negotiations will, within a year or two, have an impact on how Brewers Retail operates.

In the mid-1980s, the president of Brewers Retail was asked by this writer whether, apart from legal obligations, a sense of fair play might lead the company to allow small brewers to buy equity in the retail monopoly. The president's reply was: "Certainly not. Our first obligation is to the financial interests of our present shareholders."

While the decision-making structure of Brewers Retail is patently unfair, one might think that a large retail monopoly could at least provide knowledgeable service to the public. Such is not the case, as beerdrinking Ontarians know all too well.

Few employees of Brewers Retail know *anything* about beer other than the names of the brands they sell. Few employees know anything about brewing methods, aging time or conditioning, adjuncts and additives, beer styles, appropriate beers for given meals—the list is long. Why this should be so is puzzling.

Try to imagine a government-sanctioned monopoly which retails hardware. No other retailers are allowed to compete with The Hardware Store. Now, try to imagine this: few of the employees in this hardware monopoly know the difference between a saw and a scythe, or a bolt and a hammer. The employees in this store are very well paid, but few know anything of importance about the goods they sell, and for the most part, they don't care. Hard to imagine, isn't it?

Cynics might point out that the less Brewers Retail employees know about beer, the better it is for the large brewers. The more beer is presented as a generic product, differentiated only by price, the better it is for large brewers. The more the public knows about beer variety and beer quality, the better it is for quality-oriented brewers. If Brewers Retail had highly trained staff, they might actually converse with customers about beer ingredients, style and quality, and that might not benefit the large brewers who control Brewers Retail!

Another defect in the Brewers Retail system is its car dependency. Because beer is heavy, and because beer is not sold in corner stores, the automobile is the only real option for buying beer in most of Ontario. Brewers Retail has eliminated its home delivery service. People without cars, people like students and pensioners, are obliged to take taxis to get beer wherever public transit is inconvenient or non-existent.

In the past, when Ontario beer prices went up, Brewers Retail liked to point out that Ontario "still" had the cheapest beer prices in the country. In fact, this was occasionally a false claim. At least twice when this claim was made, beer was selling for less in Quebec. But the claim is misleading anyway.

When Brewers Retail talks about the price of beer, it ignores the cost of transportation, the cost you must pay every time you drive or take a taxi to out-of-the-way Brewers Retail outlets. Brewers Retail is willing to pass this cost on to the beerdrinker, but not willing to tally in this cost when it boasts about cheap beer prices. In fact, when transportation costs are included, it's easy to see why Brewers Retail costs most consumers more than would a corner-store system.

Brewers Retail likes to boast that with all its faults, at least it delivers the goods. This isn't quite true for many Ontarians. For many of us, Brewers Retail stores provide a pretty thin selection of Ontario's own beer. People in Ottawa, Pembroke, Sault Ste. Marie, Kingston and many other cities sometimes have to drive hundreds of kilometres just to find the Ontario beer they want.

Poor distribution of brewed-in-Ontario beer is due in part to Brewers Retail's "new brands listing fee," a charge for each new brand sold, for each package size, for each beer store in which it is sold. This fee makes it more expensive for new (and cash-strapped) breweries to sell beer than for established breweries. Because the fee applies only to new brands or new listings, it makes operating costs for new brewers higher than for established brewers, and may discourage new brewers from entering the Ontario market.

When Brewers Retail introduced its new brands listing fee, Richard Davidson, who was then in charge of Brewers Retail, said: "We simply have to have some means of *controlling the number of brands that are offered*" (emphasis added)! He continued: "We are asking a [new] brewer to be very careful about the number of brands he makes....What we're trying to do is indicate that we no longer have the privilege of giving Ontario brewers unfettered access to the system." (CBC Radio March 10, 1989). The current management at

Brewers Retail have also indicated that they would like to reduce the number of brands sold at The Beer Store.

"Controlling" the number of brands. Access to the retail monopoly as a "privilege." Mr. Davidson's remarks typify Brewers Retail's attitude toward consumers and competition: both are a bother.

Brewers Retail is so far removed from a service-oriented, consumer-pleasing philosophy that it doesn't even sell single bottles of beer! You have to buy six bottles of beer, or twelve, or eighteen. You can't buy one, or four, or ten. Quite simply, Brewers Retail is a lousy retailer. As CAMRA Canada's *What's Brewing* reported, "How does an organization like Ontario's Brewers Retail deal with dipping sales and rising costs? Well...they move to crush the competition" and "reduce basic service....He who makes the Golden makes the rules."

The Brewers Retail system is so unfair, one is tempted to ask why there hasn't been a consumer revolt—a beer-drinkers' rebellion on the grounds of Queens Park. Part of the reason is that few Ontario beerdrinkers know who owns and controls Brewers Retail. Its stores are so drab and ugly many people assume that they must be government stores. As bad as all this is, Brewers Retail has actually got worse of late. Brewers Retail permanently closed 39 stores recently, further reducing their level of service.

As Jeffrey Simpson said in *The Globe and Mail*, "What more defines the average Canadian's weekend than running the empties back to some dismal place in a suburban shopping centre? The tolerance which defines the Canadian culture has far less to do with the weather than with accepting the endless frustration of trying to find a beer store open when you really need one....Scrap the way we market beer and you might just as well abolish the Canadian Senate."

Now, as Brewers Retail faces the prospect of selling out-of-province beers, we will see whether real reform will occur. Surveys show that most Ontarians want beer to be sold in corner or grocery stores. Given Brewers Retail's track record, however, reform will not happen simply because the public wants a better system. Reform just might occur, however, if an out-of-province brewer decides that the current decision-making structure is unfair, and pursues legal remedies.

Despite its many faults, we would like to see Brewers Retail continue, but in a radically altered form. Given its size and monopoly powers, the public—not Molson and Labatt—should own Brewers Retail, preferably not through government ownership, but on a broadly held common shares basis. The decision-making structure must change so that the interests of consumers are protected. The fee structure must be made fairer. Minimum service levels must be instituted. Mandatory training programs focusing on employee beer knowledge must be introduced. Beer should be sold in single bottles. And finally, Brewers Retail should lose its monopoly status. It should face competition in the form of grocery and corner store beer sales.

The LCBO

In theory, Ontario beerdrinkers have an alternative to Brewers Retail: the Liquor Control Board of Ontario, which sells about 5% of the beer in Ontario. And indeed, the LCBO is a different kind of outlet. It is a state, as opposed to a private, monopoly. Some people might think that state monopolies are somehow more open and accountable than privately controlled monopolies, but the LCBO is neither open nor accountable, as dozens of scandals over the years have shown.

The "tainted wine" scandal showed the LCBO to be highly incompetent at the one thing it should be able to do: assure the quality of the alcohol it sells. By 1986, the LCBO had known for five years about the presence of a potential carcinogen in some of the wines it sold, but did nothing about it. Then-Attorney General Ian Scott told reporters that his ministry had considered laying charges of "negligence leading to injury and corrupt practices such as bribery" against the LCBO at this time. According to evidence given to the commission which investigated the scandal, the chairman, William Bosworth, swore some of his senior officials to secrecy regarding the potential carcinogens, but in his testimony to the commission, Mr. Bosworth denied this.

Scandals continue to abound in the LCBO's internal operations according to the most recent report of the Provincial Auditor. These include cost overruns in new buildings ($3 million in one year alone at the Whitby warehouse), missing inventory, employees being paid for "golf days," sports events and travel for social purposes (one employee was recently given $260 for travel while on vacation, according to the Auditor's report).

During the 1985 beer lockout, when the LCBO refused to bring in Canadian out-of-province beer despite a shortage of Ontario beer, Mr. Justice Robert Reid castigated the LCBO, a "non-accountable monopoly," for operating "above the law," making "decisions without any apparent concern for the welfare of their customers" or "indeed *against* the interest of their customers." For example, the LCBO could have easily "imported" beer from another province, Justice Reid noted, but it arbitrarily decided not to: "Nor are [tavern owners] entitled to know *why* those decisions were made, or why the Board's decisions are made at any time." Justice Reid characterized this as "arbitrary and untrammelled power." More than one analyst concluded that the LCBO acted the way it did—so clearly against the interests of the general public—because the large brewers wanted the LCBO to act this way.

In terms of how it retails its beer, the LCBO has a number of similarities with Brewers Retail.

Few LCBO clerks know anything about beer. Only 40 (of 621) LCBO stores in the province have "product experts"—i.e., salesclerks with some knowledge of the products they sell—on the premises.

Beer is poorly stored, seldom refrigerated, and often shelved directly under destructive fluorescent light.

Together with warm storage, storing beer under fluorescent light is one of the worst possible things one can do to beer, but this practice is still widespread at the LCBO. Why do the people at the LCBO, who should be storage experts, do such a bad job of this simple responsibility? (If you don't mind wrecking a good beer, you can discover for yourself the effects of light on beer by trying this experiment. Get two quality beers fresh out of the carton, especially beers in light-coloured bottles, and place one in a dark corner of your cellar and the other close to and directly under a fluorescent light. After ten days, compare the taste of the two beers. You'll be surprised at the difference.)

In addition to storing beer in a quality-reducing fashion, the LCBO knowingly sells less-than-fresh beer. A recent (May, 1992) memo from LCBO head office tells LCBO store managers : "Please note that [the] 'freshness date' is *not* an expiry date. Store managers should not mark down any [stale] American beer...." The LCBO could, but doesn't, tell beer buyers that a given shipment of beer is past its best-before date.

The LCBO generally restricts its imported beer sales to six packs, a silly, anti-competitive restriction likely to be changed under GATT promptings. The LCBO limits its domestic beer sales to one brand per brewer.

For beer aficionados, one of the LCBO's worst characteristics is its unwillingness to sell a decent selection of imported beer. Although the LCBO is one of the largest importers and handlers of alcohol in the world, it does not provide much beer variety. The LCBO limits its beer sales almost exclusively to mainstream, fast-selling beers. This is efficient for the LCBO, needless to say, but an insult to its captive clients. A private store can sell what it wants; a monopoly has an obligation to provide a broad selection.

Many small, independently owned alcohol stores in the U.S. and Europe sell five or ten times the number of brands of imported beer sold by the LCBO. One store in Rochester, New York, for example, sells seven to eight hundred different brands of beer. The average LCBO sells ten to fifteen brands. Is the LCBO trying to encourage cross-border shopping? Small cafés and bars in Belgium and Holland often stock ten or even twenty times the number of beers sold by the entire LCBO.

Just as important: many privately owned beer stores in the U.S. and Europe sell brands from ten or fifteen different beer *styles*. A "good" LCBO typically sells beer from four or five styles.

As a monopoly, the LCBO has no incentive to provide variety, but this problem is aggravated by the fact that the LCBO's listing policy is "supplier-driven." LCBO listings are generally the result of a supplier's initiative, a supplier determined enough to put up with the LCBO's long and onerous "product listing" and "product management" procedures. Many out-of-province brewers consider the LCBO to be extremely difficult to deal with. Listings almost never occur as a result of consumer interest. Over the years, we have suggested twenty or thirty interesting, marketable beers for the LCBO to sell; none of them have been listed. The LCBO's beer listings do not reflect what beerdrinkers want to drink; they reflect the determination of a few suppliers to jump through various hoops set up by the Liquor Board.

For those of us who get tired of the Becks-Corona-Bass line at the LCBO, the Liquor Board will, in theory, obtain a foreign beer through its "Private Stock" department. Unfortunately, this theory is almost never born out in practice. Far too often, the Private Stock department is unable to obtain beers that are freely available in the U.S. and Europe. Often it takes Private Stock months just to respond to a request, only to say that it cannot obtain the requested beer.

An additional responsibility that you'd think a state monopoly would be able to handle fairly well is that of regulating the breweries. In fact, this is largely the responsibility of the LCBO's sister organization, the LLBO. Despite evidence over a fifty year period that large brewers were using inducements to secure sales—one of the gravest infractions of the liquor laws, and a practice that can result in the loss of licence—the LLBO has never taken away a single brewer's licence. In fact, despite having evidence from the Ontario Provincial Police and independent auditors that kickbacks were common in the early and mid-1980s, the LLBO took no action. Illegal inducements tend to reduce competition, and are especially hard on small brewers. For the public, the result is reduced choice.

"Breweries admit paying illegal kickbacks" headlined the *Toronto Star* in a 1986 story on the practice. "Just walk into any hotel or tavern and don't be surprised if you find only one company's draught available. Or you might find some company noticeably absent," said the vice-president of Molson Ontario Breweries in the *Toronto Star* story. "That means somebody has got to somebody. It's been going on for years."

And the illegal practices continue today. In the past three or four years, the LLBO could have taken away Labatt's and Molson's licence to make and sell beer for various similar infractions of the liquor laws but, having done nothing for so long, the LLBO has decided to start enforcing the laws by slapping brewers' wrists instead. Starting in 1989, the LLBO has intermittently required Labatt and Molson to make some modest donations to charities for a variety of illegal promotional practices.

The LLBO also seems to do its job of regulating beer advertising very poorly. At the same time that the LLBO permits the mindless beer ads we see on TV, it treats freedom of speech in a cavalier fashion. When the Detroit brewer Stroh tried to place advertisements in five Ontario newspapers, the LLBO forbade the publishing of the advertisements. The ads complained that certain Ontario brewers had pressured the province into raising the price of imported beer. The LLBO prohibited Stroh from putting this message before the public. The LLBO, a non-elected body headed by a political appointee, chose to keep Ontarians in the dark about a matter of great public import. As *The Globe and Mail* noted, "In Ontario, free speech suffers along with beer drinkers."

Like Brewers Retail, the LCBO's faults are the natural result of its monopoly position and its lack of consumer focus. As *The Globe and Mail* has noted, "The hierarchy of liquor in Ontario is a fearful thing. It wields power without accountability and jeopardizes businesses without a second thought." We would argue that even were the LCBO better run, it would still not likely match the service, the variety and customer orientation that one customarily finds in a private beer store. The LCBO should be radically over-hauled and have many of its monopoly functions given to the private sector.

The big brewers

The story of Molson and Labatt is in many ways the story of Canadian economic protectionism. For almost as long as they've been in business, Molson and Labatt (and until recently, Carling-O'Keefe, formerly Canadian Breweries) have sought protection from competition in the beer market.

Above, we have reviewed some of the problems at the Brewers Retail monopoly. In the 1930s, small brewers like the Heuther brewery of Kitchener complained that E. P. Taylor and his large brewery (now part of the Molson family) were using Brewers Retail to squeeze them out of business. Something of the essence of Mr. Taylor's attitudes toward trade practices can be gained from looking at a letter he wrote to the Premier of the time: "I told [the brewer] that if the matter was not settled this week, our company would have to engage in a price war to regain our position and either put our competitors out of business or make them so groggy that they will behave." You can almost smell the smoke from E.P.'s cigar and hear him rub his hands.

While protection allowed the big brewers to prosper, Ontario beerdrinkers have paid a heavy price. Even today, beerdrinkers continue to pay for the minimal beer competition in Ontario. As the Bureau of Competition Policy stated in their "backgrounder" to the approval of the Molsons-Elders merger: "regulation in Ontario effectively eliminates price competition among the major domestic brewing companies [but] they still compete in respect of nonprice dimensions such as promotion" (!!!).

In arguing for protection from foreign competition, the large brewers have often used the "economies of scale" argument. They say that if American brewers had unfettered access to the Canadian market, America could swamp us with cheap, assembly-line suds. There's always that story about the mothballed brewery somewhere in Ohio that is so big, so automated, and so efficient (efficient, apparently, but mothballed) that it alone could supply the entire Canadian beer market. Unfortunately, this argument tends to work against the large Canadian brewers over the long run. Even now, as Molson and Labatt complain about a "flat" beer market, these two brewers are largely suffering from a problem of their own making.

For when they speak of economies of scale, they are essentially saying that beer is a generic product—that price is the only factor considered by beer consumers when faced with a choice. If they believe that price—not flavour or quality—is the key factor which distinguishes one beer from another, then their brewing philosophy will be governed by a relentless drive to lower costs at the expense of quality. This philosophy is based on the premise that most beer-drinkers will gladly drink low-quality beer to save money. In fact, many beerdrinkers *will* choose the cheapest product, given a choice, but we believe that it is a mistake for Labatt or Molson to chase the low end of the market.

In an open and competitive marketplace, undifferentiated products will find it difficult or impossible to compete. To find and defend a market niche, a product must respond to a specific population's notions of quality. Not to the *average* of a large number of populations, but to a specific population. Think, for example, about how clothing is designed and marketed. Or wine. Or tourist destinations. Or think about cars.

It has taken North American car makers a long time to learn a simple marketplace fact, but eventually, and painfully, they have. They learned that they could not be everything to everybody, and they learned that by gearing so much production to the fictional average consumer, they made a third-rate car that nobody really wanted. Increasingly, the large North American automakers are engineering and marketing high-quality cars for smaller groups of people based on their real transport needs (like getting to out-of-the-way Beer Stores). The North American car-makers won't reach all of the people all of the time. But they will find their niches, and if they sell a good product to those niches, they will prosper.

Molson and Labatt need to learn a similar lesson. They need to learn something about quality and product differentiation, about market niches and making the best product of a given type in the world. They need to lose their arrogance. They need to treat their customers with some respect.

We cannot, however, expect large commercial breweries to think that a sudden conversion to brewing all-malt real ale, or short-run specialty beers, is in their best short-or long-term interest. To date, their bottom line has been reasonably well served by brewing and marketing "inoffensive" mass market beer. But large brewers must eventually realize that their best long-term interests are served by defining, in terms of uniqueness and quality, who they are and what they brew. That is, they need a mission statement related to beer.

Most large commercial breweries in North America have a sense of mission. But it seems obvious that this sense of mission has more to do with earning profit than with brewing the best possible beer, or educating the beerdrinking public about beer style. The mission statement for many large brewers would seem to be "Get a better ad agency than the competition. Save money on ingredients. Increase marketshare by advertising relentlessly and marketing aggressively. Increase profit."

Most beerdrinkers can remember a time when Canadian beer was noticeably, even dramatically, better than American beer; it was one of the few things we knew we did better than the Americans did. We knew it, and so did Americans who had tried our beer. It was a cliche you'd hear from visiting Americans: "Ah Canada! Great wilderness and great beer." Here's Thomas Wolfe on Canadian beer in the 1920s: Montreal is four-fifths imitation American and one-fifth imitation English, but the beer and ale were splendidly real!" That was some time ago.

There was a reason for the remarkably better quality of Canadian beer. American commercial brewers, long before the practice became widespread in Canada, used ever greater quantities of adjuncts, making an ever cheaper—and ever blander—product. While Americans were getting used to the taste of fermented rice, Canadian drinkers were still buying beer that was essentially made from malted barley. Not often Reinheitsgebot pure, but recognizably beer.

Top-selling beer brands in Canada (1992)

1.	Labatt Blue	6.	Carling O'Keefe
2.	Molson Golden	7.	Coors brands
3.	Molson Export	8.	Molson Special Dry
4.	Budweiser	9.	Laurentide
5.	Labatt 50	10.	Old Vienna

source: The Globe and Mail

But in the past twenty years the big brewers (especially Molson, we believe) have reduced the malt and hops in many of their beers, and they have increased the level of adjunct, primarily corn. That is to say, they have made their beer cheaper, blander, and more like the "Wet Air" sold widely in the U.S.

The large Canadian brewers have hastened the Americanization of Canadian beer by introducing a number of American brands brewed under licence. As the chart above shows, Budweiser and Coors have done particularly well. The introduction of American brands was motivated by Molson's and Labatt's desire to increase marketshare, and the licensing agreements were attractive to the American partners as well because the Americans were unable to gain fair market access in Canada, particularly in the key Ontario market.

The Canadian versions of American brands were perhaps less the result of real consumer demand for American beer than the inevitable result of unfair trade practices at home. The very inability of Canadians to buy American beer in a normal fashion may have artificially stimulated demand for what was (and in many ways, still is), a generally inferior product.

The Americanization of Canadian brands has different roots but equally negative consequences. Perhaps the greatest impetus to change in Canadian brands in the past twenty years has been the big brewers' desire to have the greatest number of "national brands," brands which will offend the least number of people, which are susceptible to image manipulation, particularly on TV.

The big brewers have been "chasing the centre," eliminating the hard, identifiable edges of flavour, striving to produce an alcoholic, gassy product which would be so free from distinction that one could drink it without noticing the taste. That this "chase to the centre" also happens to produce cheaper, and sometimes more profitable beer (most adjuncts are cheaper than malted barley) may be coincidental, but we don't think so. The result is that Molson's and Labatt's beers are now much more American than they were in the 1950s: more insipid, much less bitter (the result of lower levels of "bittering hops"), and with fewer dark, complex flavours.

Consequently most Molson and Labatt products in this huge, diverse country are now virtually indistinguishable from one another. It's to the point where even different *styles* of beer are hard to distinguish. As Brian Edwards, director of public relations at Carling-O'Keefe said in the mid-1980s: "Ales and lagers are so similar now, it's hard to tell the difference between them. Maybe it was possible 25 years ago but not now. I don't think anyone tasting an ale and a lager blind-folded could distinguish between them." What Mr. Edwards means, of course, is that no one can tell the difference between a big brewer ale and a big brewer lager. As an ex-employee of a large brewery said to *Canadian Consumer:* the major national brands are actually just "various degrees of water."

Any beer lover can tell the difference—blindfolded—between Wellington County Ale and Creemore Springs Lager. Ten times out of ten. Or between Brick Premium Lager and Conners Ale. Or between any number of authentic ales and lagers. When employees of the large breweries say that ales and lagers are indistinguishable, one wonders whether they have ever drunk quality beer.

The large brewers have added to the "they-all-taste-the-same" problem by dropping their smaller, often unadvertised brands from production. Often these brands have had distinguishable taste, and occasionally a degree of quality. Molson's Porter was killed in 1991, an example of a distinctive brand (and of reasonable quality, we thought), sent to the graveyard for daring to be different, for having character and flavour. One Molson employee told us that Porter was "too expensive to make."

There is every evidence that at Molson, at least, cutting corners and blandification will continue. According to *The Globe and Mail*, one of Molson's strategies for the 1990s is to further "reduce [the] cost of barley," and to "cut back on product lines."

Labatt and Molson need to learn the poignant lesson presented by the decline of the formerly successful Joseph Schlitz Brewing Company. In 1978, Schlitz brewed 13 million barrels of beer. In 1984, Schlitz was only brewing 1.8 million barrels, an 86% drop, worth tens of millions of dollars.

The reason? The substitution of corn syrup for barley malt and a perceptible decline in quality. As a retired Schlitz manager said, "Schlitz sacrificed its reputation in...pursuit of bigger profits. In the beer business, if a company loses its resources and money, but retains its reputation, it can always be rebuilt. But if it loses its reputation, no amount of money and resources will bring it back" ("Whatever Happened To..." by David A. Aaker, in *Across the Board*, April 1992). The lesson of Schlitz is that a large brewery can go into a tailspin as it loses sight of quality. Are Molson and Labatt losing long-term viability as they pursue short-term profit?

The Americanization and the increasing sameness of Big Two beers is the result of the manufacturing mentality, of the fact that bottom-liners, not brewers, are in charge. It is also the result of Labatt and Molson having a rather low estimation of the drinking public.

Together, Molson and Labatt spend over $100 million dollars a year on...hops?...barley research? La fat chance.

Advertising, old chum. Advertising relentlessly, expensively, and usually quite offensively. In a large brewery, the vice-president of marketing is a pretty important guy (they always seem to be men). Far more important than the head brewer or the quality control chief. If you've never met one of these extremely important people, perhaps you will learn something by listening to one as he speaks: "Blue has experienced some recent softness. It has added some greyness, lost some crispness," (*The Globe and Mail*). Got it?

We didn't make this up. That was a Labatt vice-president of marketing talking about their number one seller. Here's the chairman of an advertising agency characterizing beerdrinkers as he sees them: "We are talking testosterone here. Rock and roll and girls. Not a lot of these guys read *Finnegan's Wake* or are into Hegelian dialectics."

We would wager that beerdrinkers read more Joyce and Hegel than do ad execs, but aside from that, we take keen interest in the attitude: most beerdrinkers are uncultured, adolescent morons. The use of attractive, empty-headed women to pitch beer to empty-headed men is so deeply engrained in the mentality of some brewers, they even have a name for it: the "T & A factor," or the "jiggly-wigglies." Charming.

Many people have criticized the TV beer advertisements of the big brewers. The sexism, the mind-numbing stupidity, and the use of "lifestyle" to sell beer have all come under attack. Another pertinent criticism can also be made.

Few of the ads address the most important aspects of the beers they are supposed to be "informing" you about: ingredients, ageing time, brewing method, or style. Most ads have little of the basic and relevant information that an informed beerdrinker would seek. The regulations governing beer advertising are partly to blame, but so are the large brewers themselves. While Labatt's and Molson's ads have become less blatantly sexist of late, they still imply that beerdrinkers are enormously stupid. The big brewers' demographic profile of their main buyer seems to be that of a white, middle class, sexually insecure and intellectually impoverished good-time boy. Selling to this market, the ads imply that beerdrinkers care more about social conformity and a purchasable image than they do about quality, beer style, ingredients or brewing method. After decades of this insulting advertising, it's a wonder that beerdrinkers don't mirror the demographic profile the ads tried to create!

A two hundred million dollar increase for *what*?

	1980	1990	% Increase
Barley malt	$97,000,000	$131,000,000	35.05
Bottles and cans	$60,000,000	$267,000,000	445.00
Cartons and labels	$111,000,000	$164,000,000	47.75

source: Brewers Association of Canada

The figures above (national, not provincial) tell an interesting story. Given that the Big Two brewers brew about 95%

of the beer sold in Canada, these statistics tell us much about the values of the brewing giants, as well as the costs they incur.

In 1980, brewers spent a good deal more on barley malt than they did on bottles and cans—about 60% more. Ten years later, brewers spent *more than twice as much on bottles and cans as they did on malt, the key ingredient in beer!*

Who paid for the $200 million, or 445%, increase in bottle and can costs? Need we say it? Beerdrinkers paid for every bit of it. We paid in money, or we paid in reduced beer quality. In beer, there is no free lunch. (Interestingly, the expression "There's no such thing as a free lunch" has its roots in beer. In an attempt to drum up lucrative midday business, British pubs used to advertise "Free Lunch!" or "Buy two pints and get a free lunch!" The expression was a reaction to these signs.)

The monstrous increase in packaging costs can be attributed largely to the brewing giants' ongoing packaging wars and bottle redesigns. Painted bottles don't come cheap. The staggering cost of these packaging wars is the major reason Molson and Labatt are now moving back to a standardized bottle. Ironically, it was largely the large brewers themselves who got themselves into this mess: they lobbied successfully to eliminate mandatory use of the old standardized bottle, the "stubby." They wanted, they said, to "differentiate" their beers by putting them into differently shaped bottles.

Some analysts believe that there are more sinister motives at work in the current push for a standardized bottle. The cost of changing bottles is very, very expensive. New bottles must be bought; the bottling line must be refit or a new one installed. Other packaging costs are also involved: label design, label application, case packaging, etc. In addition, there are brand loyalty and advertising implications. Given these huge costs, a mandatory standardized bottle may put a few smaller brewers out of business.

This would appear to be the whole point: Labatt and

Molson, who have had about forty different bottle designs between them, would save huge sums of money, even as crippling new financial burdens are foisted onto the small brewers, who are increasingly seen as serious competition. Analysts have also noted that such a move would be a way to circumvent fair trade rules by making it harder for imports to meet bottling regulations.

So now that the big brewers have Americanized the Canadian beer scene—and in the process degraded the quality of a formerly respectable product as well as "educated" the public that adjuncts, chemicals, and image advertising are what beer is all about— now that they've brought about this state of affairs, how sorry should we feel for these brewers as they complain about a "flat" beer market and diminishing marketshare? Now that they have Canadians used to the taste of pap, why should we sympathize with Molson or Labatt if Canadians decide to get their pap at the cheapest possible price? Indeed, why would any beerdrinker buy imitation Wet Air when she or he can get the real McCoy, genuine American Wet Air, for a few pennies less? Surely the big brewers don't expect sympathy from their long-suffering, previously captive clientele?

It seems to us that Molson and Labatt—by making their beers more insipid and more alike, and by reducing the level of public education about beer through offensive advertising and through their refusal to divulge ingredients—have created a horrifying dilemma for themselves as low-end American beer gains greater access to our market. The large brewers, most especially Molson, have squandered a great advantage: the reputation of superiority that Canadian beer has enjoyed vis-à-vis American beer. This is a terrific loss, a sad waste of an important "goodwill" asset.

The big brewers, like Brewers Retail and the LCBO, show little interest in changing their ways. The brands and the advertising change, but the same shoddy attitude persists. We can only hope that the large brewers regain an interest in beer as an exciting and interesting beverage. We dearly hope that the large brewers experience an about-face in attitude and mission. If they do, we will all be the better for it. If they do not, we can only hope that their influence over retailing does not drag the smaller breweries down with them.

3
UNDERSTANDING AND APPRECIATING BEER

"And malt does more than Milton can
To justify God's ways to man"
— A. E. Housman

What is good beer?

What's a "good" beer? Is it possible to say that a beer is "good," "fair" or "bad"?

Isn't every beer good? There are two ways to grapple with this; both are valid; both need to be qualified.

One school of thought says that beer is good if the person drinking it says it's good: "good" is purely subjective. To the question "What makes a beer good?" the answer is "My say-so!" When people say "This is a good beer," what they're really saying is that they like it.

Another school of thought says that certain objective factors come into play in defining a good beer. This line of thinking would say that beer is good if it meets certain objectively defined criteria. These criteria, or properties, could even be analyzed and quantified for various beer styles. In fact, a number of quantitative measures have developed over the years, mostly to help the commercial brewers as they develop a new brand, or perform their quality control. Colour, bitterness, and density are three of beer's key properties which have their own numeric systems of description.

"Beer is good if the person drinking it says it's good." There is an undeniable truth in this proposition. The proposition is especially appealing to beerdrinkers who view the beer world as inherently more democratic and less snobbish than the world of wine, or single malt scotch. And, after all, beer is meant to be enjoyed.

There's no point arguing with Joe who thinks his Holland Marsh Lite Lager is the best beer in the world. Joe, like the drinker in *The Pickwick Papers*, would happily ask for "a double glass o' the inwariable." And there's no point arguing with Jane who thinks her Muskoka Pure All Malt Brown Ale is the best beer in the world either. *"Chacun à son goût."* Beer is meant to be enjoyed. An enjoyable beer is a good beer.

This democratic attitude needs some qualification, however. First, few Canadians, and fewer still who call for a "double glass o' the inwariable," have tried even one percent of the world's six to ten thousand different beers. Few Canadians have tried even half of the more than twenty distinct beer styles. So if Joe and Jane are typical Canadians, perhaps we should take their claims about the "best" beers with a grain of salt. Joe may like his Holland Marsh Lite Lager, and he probably believes it to be "good." It would be more accurate to say that Holland Marsh Lite appeals to him, that it appeals to him more at this time than the other brands that he has actually tried. Likewise, Jane's claim that Muskoka Pure All Malt Brown Ale is "the best beer in the world" is a tenuous claim based on inadequate data. Still, for Joe and Jane, these two beers are good.

Second, beer is more than a matter of taste. Even taste is more than a matter of taste. Beer taste is shaped by beer knowledge, and there is a lot of beer knowledge to be had. Many beer lovers start their life-long beer odyssey drinking whatever is at hand (filched from Dad, maybe), and then try a few of their friends' favourite brands, and then, often on their first trip abroad, start to experience the extraordinary range and variety that beer has to offer.

"Good beer can be objectively defined." To a large extent, good beer can be defined outside the realm of subjectivity. Good beer should be brewed only from the best ingredients, and good beer should be properly aged or conditioned, and then (in all but a few cases) served "fresh," as soon as it is ready, which is when beer is at its peak. An important way to get a handle on the ingredient aspect of goodness is to keep in mind the Reinheitsgebot, the beer purity law which stipulates that beer be made only from malted barley, hops, and water.

The Reinheitsgebot goes back to sixteenth-century Bavaria, 1516 to be exact. Yeast, which is not an ingredient so much as a catalyst, was not mentioned in the original legislation. Its properties were unknown at the time—beer fermented "spontaneously" with the aid of wild yeast—but cultured yeast is now deemed an acceptable, indeed a necessary, part of the brewing process.

While the Reinheitsgebot law lost a little of its force after it was challenged as a "trade barrier" in the European Court, all beer brewed for domestic consumption in Germany, and virtually all beer drunk by Germans, is still Reinheitsgebot beer. Germans are so used to drinking good beer that German visitors have been known to gag and spew—literally—on trying their first industrial beer from North America.

But what influence can an ancient German purity law have on the beers brewed in Ontario? A good deal, we think.

First, it remains a standard for many brewers; it is part of beer's ethic and culture. Second, it can be a guarantee of purity and excellence for drinkers. As people become more concerned about the safety and nutritive value of comestibles and potables, they look for guarantees that the products they put in their stomachs are pure and natural. The Reinheitsgebot is such a guarantee. This kind of assurance is especially important for beer. Beer sold in Canada need not list its ingredients, and some brewers actually refuse to reveal what ingredients in addition to malt, water and hops they use. The fact that brewers can refuse to divulge ingredients put into a potable product is shocking when you consider that by law, pet food lists ingredients.

Why are beerdrinkers not given the same respect that pet food manufacturers give goldfish, toads and parakeets?

In Ontario, quite a few beers now meet the Reinheitsgebot standard. Generally a beer that is Reinheitsgebot pure will say so directly or indirectly, e.g., "contains malt, hops and water only." We like the term Reinheitsgebot because, unlike "all natural ingredients," or "no preservatives," it is precise.

"All natural ingredients" often means that malted barley has been supplemented by "adjunct," a cheaper, less flavourful source of sugars with the potential to convert to alcohol. Even glucose and dextrose can be considered "natural." Corn and rice are two of the more common adjuncts. Sometimes adjuncts are used to obtain desired technical properties. Wheat, both malted and unmalted, is often used to enhance head retention and lighten the body of beer, and fruit and spices can be wonderful non-malt ingredients. But most often adjuncts are used to save the brewer money. Malted barley costs more, sometimes much more, than most adjuncts.

Beer brewed with adjunct—up to 25% or so—is not *necessarily* bad. Indeed, as the ratings show, we like several beers with adjunct, e.g., Hart Amber Ale, more than some all-malt beers. Beer need not always be Reinheitsgebot to be good, but a Reinheitsgebot beer is always a beer worthy of serious consideration. Reinheitsgebot beer is often good beer simply by virtue of being brewed from 100% barley malt. Wet Air, the low-end suds from the U.S., is up to 65% adjunct! "Carbonated corn product," or "fizzy rice drink" would be a more accurate description of this stuff. Bad beer can be objectively defined—any beer with more than 30-33% adjunct (excluding wheat) is almost certain to be awful.

"Beer is good if the person drinking it says it's good" versus "good beer as objectively defined": this is a serious matter, worthy of much pub debate.

One important consideration in addressing this matter is

the *context* of the beer at hand. This context can include: food or drink taken immediately before tasting a beer; the health and mood of the drinker; the ambience in which the beer is drunk; the knowledge and open-mindedness of the drinker; the season, the temperature and the time of the day; expectations of the drinker; the temperature and the freshness of the beer; and the way the beer is poured and the glass it is served in. Context is *very* important, and obviously quite a few aspects need to be considered.

One of the most interesting aspects of the beerdrinking context is the time of the year and the beer's seasonal suitability. One of beer's delights is its relationship to season. An anonymous poet once wrote:

> *My love in her attire doth show her wit*
> *It doth so well become her*
> *For every season she hath dressings fit*
> *For winter, spring and summer*

It seems clear that the poet's love was beer, and that the verse is a paean to the seasonal styles of beer. (The poet lived in an autumn-less clime.) Beer has seasonal aspects, but thoughtful beerdrinkers sometimes disagree as to which beer styles are most suitable to given seasons.

We think that spring's particular seasonal pleasure is to be found in slightly sweet bocks, dark lagers, bitters and medium-bodied pale ales. On the first truly hot day of the year, a sunny and memorable joy is opening a first-rate pilsner or Dortmunder style lager, breathing in the hoppy nose, and sipping out of a tall pilsner glass. We like a dry brown ale on summer evenings. In fall, we like Viennas, bitters and malty ales. Winter's beers—well aged, higher gravity ales, porters, stouts and winter bocks—are best drunk by a fire or in the warmth of a friendly pub.

For many summer worshippers, lager is the style of choice right from planting days in May to first harvest in late August. Having Pilsner Urquell in constant supply may be the LCBO's greatest service to Ontarians. Upper Canada Lager, Brick Premium, Creemore Springs, Labatt Classic, Sleeman's Lager and Niagara Falls Trapper are all fine summer lagers, just the thing for camping or reading the newspaper in a lawnchair.

Many ale fans respond to the idea of summer by drinking ales that are either low in gravity (like Wellington's Arkell Best Bitter) or dry in finish (like Labatt's IPA). Mildly bitter Sleeman's Cream Ale also complements summer's heat and langour. Such ales, lightly chilled, are a great way to turn a barbecued hot dog into an aristocratic meal. Of course the most important summer element for beerdrinkers is summer itself— that, and local setting. What pleasure can match the drinking of a favourite beer on a deck at a cottage, at a campsite by a fire, or on a terrace shaded by a tall tree at a well-run pub or hotel?

Having a good supply of winter beer at hand can take some of the tedium out of a long, gruelling winter. Brick's bock, Conners' Imperial stout, and Wellington's Iron Duke strong ale are surely reason enough to stay here and skip Florida. We also like malty lagers like Upper Canada's Rebellion on a snowy day.

While some of the smaller brewers try to respond to the demands and associations of season, Brewers Retail's fee system does not encourage the brewing of seasonal beers. Consequently, few seasonal beers are brewed in Ontario.

We can let season influence our drinking, however. Upper Canada's Wheat beer is a fine contribution to the wheat style, and a terrific drink for a summer afternoon, after a baseball game or a round on the links. Quebec's St. Ambroise, with wheat also added to its malts, is another great beer suggestive of summer. Live a little: into the bottom of a tulip glass pour an inch of raspberry juice and top up with Upper Canada Wheat.

Some beerdrinkers appreciate the idea of seasonal beers, but do not want to restrict their consumption to a given style or brand. These people might argue that the beerdrinker's mood, the food on the table, the time of the day, all combine to create a personal "season" that suggests the kind of beer that should be drunk at a given moment. These people would argue that any beer can be drunk at any time, that season should inspire the brewer, but not dictate to the drinker.

And who are we to argue? Each quality beer is clamouring to be drunk: "*Now* is the time to try me," these beers whisper. When we are asked, "what is your favourite beer?" we cannot provide a simple answer. Indeed, we cannot answer at all. Do you mean favourite beer with a tandoori dinner? Favourite beer after a baseball game? Favourite dessert beer after dinner? Favourite beer after skiing on a bitterly cold winter day? Favourite celebration beer at the end of a school term?

"Beer is good if the person drinking it says it's good" versus "good beer as objectively defined." Obviously there are many factors at play when we talk about "good beer."

Yet another factor is the variability of beer batch to batch (although most commercial brewers strive to attain consistency). Or the variability of draught beer from the start of the keg to the end of the keg (draught can be better near the beginning of the keg). Or the difference between a bottled beer and the "same" beer on tap. So much to consider. Good beer is partly a matter of taste, but to an extent, good beer can be objectively defined.

Good beer is always brewed with care, from the best ingredients—first rate barley which has been malted to precise specifications, good water (which often means water treatment); fresh, high quality hops, and rigorously maintained (for purity) yeast. Good beer is usually true to style, and the style should be noted somewhere on the packaging. Good beer is most often brewed with no adjuncts—e.g., rice and corn—although there are many exceptions. Good beer often—not always, but often—"laces" well in the glass: it leaves a beautiful, intricate lacy pattern on the side of the glass. Good beer often has a quiet head—it makes no noise as it disappears. All this is true. But ultimately, good beer for you is beer that you think is good. The more varieties of beer you drink, the more your sense of "goodness" will develop. The more your sense of goodness develops, the more you will want to try different beers: a vicious circle many people find easy to live with.

Learning about beer

Better than knowing what makes a beer good in the abstract is developing a personal understanding of the various beer styles and characteristics. Personal knowledge is the result of drinking and thinking, discussing beers with friends, reading, writing, and even brewing at home.

Learning about beer is fun. It never ends. Like learning about literature, opera, orchids, guitar-making, windmills—like any worthy pursuit—learning about beer never ends. The subject is virtually bottomless. Outlined below are a number of ways to develop your beer knowledge.

Reading. The number of books and magazines devoted to beer grows year by year. Perhaps the best introduction for most people is Michael Jackson's *New World Guide to Beer*. Jackson—the *real* Michael Jackson—is knowledgeable, and almost anything he writes on beer is worth reading and thinking about. His tastes are catholic and his passions wide-ranging. As a beer "sherpa" he is hard to beat. His columns also appear in *Zymurgy*, the American homebrewing magazine. Another Jackson book every beer lover should own is the Simon & Schuster *Pocket Guide to Beer*, an international ratings guide.

Ian Bowering's *The Art and Mystery of Brewing in Ontario* is an attractive history of beer and brewing. With dozens of fascinating photographs and many good anecdotes, the book provides a useful historical context for understanding Ontario's present beer scene.

Three good magazines are *What's Brewing* (U.K.), *Zymurgy* (American Homebrewers Association) which focuses mostly on homebrewing, and *American Brewer*.

Occasionally wine and food magazines publish interesting beer articles.

Keeping a beer notebook. Finding words to describe and record sense impressions of beer is difficult. As daunting as writing about beer can be at first, you'll discover that jotting down your thoughts about a beer will teach you a few things. You'll develop a sense of how to appreciate a given beer; you'll come to understand your own preferences; and you'll learn a good deal about what makes various beers different.

Tastings. One of the best and most enjoyable ways to learn about beer is to taste a variety of beers, usually within a style. For example, a "pale ale and bitter tasting" might include three, four or five of: Wellington County's Arkell Best Bitter and SPA, Upper Canada's Publican's Special Bitter, Molson's Stock Ale, Conners' Bitter and Ale, Labatt's IPA, and, from Vintages, one or two British pale ales or bitters. A lager tasting might include Brick's Premium, Creemore Springs, Labatt's Classic, Sleeman's Lager, and, from the LCBO, Beck's, a German lager.

In a tasting, the focus is on recording your *qualitative* impressions of a number of beers. Inevitably, you will make comparisons—"I like this one better than that one; that one is awful!"—but this is not the object. The object is to appreciate the unique characteristics of each of several beers which are stylistically similar. To record these characteristics, (and to help in making meaningful comparisons), you need some kind of sheet or notebook on which to record your impressions. A "Rating/Evaluation Sheet" is provided for this purpose in Appendix A. You can use it as is, modify it, or develop your own evaluation sheet.

Samples are typically about three ounces—enough to sip a couple of times, and then to return to for an additional sip later. "Did you ever taste beer?" "I had a sip of it once," said the small servant. "Here's a state of things!" cried Mr. Swiveller....."She never tasted it—it can't be tasted in a sip!" [*Dick Swiveller*, Charles Dickens].

Whether you are formally evaluating beer, learning about it, or simply savouring it, we suggest that you try to be aware of the factors which can influence the way a beer strikes you. Beer taste and the overall impression made by a given beer vary enormously depending on the contextual factors outlined above. Be especially aware of: amount of alcohol consumed, time of day (the sensitivity of the taste buds declines as the day wears on), shape of the glass, temperature of the beer, how the beer is poured and the size of the head, and your expectations.

Varying a beer grouping is a good way to see the importance of context. An Upper Canada Lager will make one impression when tasted with Brick Premium and Creemore Springs, and another impression when tried with Beck's and Holsten, two imports.

Joining a beer group. Beer is a wonderfully social beverage, and to develop your beer knowledge, you need to talk and to listen to other beer enthusiasts.

Beer groups are springing up across Ontario. Visit your closest homebrew supplies store for information on local beer groups. (Homebrew supplies stores can be found in the yellow pages of the phone book under "Winemaking Equipment.")

You can also form your own beer group. Put up a sign in a pub that sells a good selection of beer. You can start by meeting in the pub and holding a formal or informal tasting.

Touring a brewery. Some of the breweries listed in this guide permit or even encourage tours. But brewers are busy people, so try to phone or write ahead to make a reservation.

Breweries are enormously interesting and tours have much to offer the beer enthusiast. Many breweries also sell beer-related teeshirts, caps, glassware, etc.

Brewing your own beer. Brewing at home is a delightful and educational experience. Many people start homebrewing motivated by the cost savings. Those who keep at it tend to do it for the variety of beer flavour and the learning that homebrewing affords.

Interestingly, homebrewing can help you understand more about commercial beer. It can help you develop a sense of beer style. Brewing at home is also sure to increase your admiration for the best of the commercial brewers.

To get started, visit your local homebrew supplies store.

Taking a beer vacation. We noted above that a survey showed beer to be the main reason that Canadian tourists choose Germany as a destination. Beer tours of Belgium and Britain are also increasingly popular. The idea of beer tourism is just starting to take hold in California and the New England States—perhaps Ontario is not far behind.

A beer vacation can run along a number of different lines. It can be bicycling to rural breweries in Belgium. It can be a tour of historic pubs in Britain. It can be a visit to a beer festival in Washington State. It can be a visit to six different Toronto-area brewpubs, three per night on a weekend. It can be a few days at the huge Oktoberfest celebrations in Kitchener.

Some travel agents will help you plan beer-related tourism, but we think it fun to do our own research and preparation.

Collecting breweriana. "Breweriana" is beer-related stuff: beermats, glasses, steins, beer cans and bottles, openers, ashtrays, trays, posters and even clocks. Much of it is fascinating. Collecting breweriana is one way to develop a sense of beer history, and to develop knowledge about aspects of beer and brewing.

Brewerianists, as they are called, like to trade the items they collect. Some of these items are quite valuable; rare bottles, for example, can fetch more than $100.

For further information, contact The Canadian Brewerianist, 2978 Lakeview Trail, Brites Grove, Ontario, N0N 1C0.

Beer style in Ontario

The concept of "style" in beer is indispensable to the drinker who wants to get a handle on beer. To be able to describe and compare beers, and to know what makes beers look, taste and smell the way they do, you need to know something about style— the major distinctive groups within the great family of beers.

You also need to know about style in order to compare one beer with another. You don't compare Ian's apple cider with Eleanor's lemonade: they're different drinks, and have to be treated on their own merits. Likewise it is more useful to compare Northern Breweries Northern ale with Molson Export ale than with Labatt's Velvet Cream Porter, which is also an ale, but of a different style.

Many Ontario beerdrinkers are completely unaware of style but we can hardly blame them. Advertisements for mass market beer seldom mention style. And, until recently, the few remaining examples of style other than the "Canadian ale" and the "international lager" styles were disappearing in Ontario. The result is a beerdrinking generation that knows less about beer style than the preceding one. This problem is underscored when you hear people complain that "American beer" is cheaper than "Canadian beer." As if beer were a generic product. You'd never hear people complain that a beaujolais costs more than a table wine; with wine and beer and many things in life, you get what you pay for. Each beer should be seen as an example of a style. To compare beer solely on the basis of price is, well, ignorant.

How many beer styles are there? Some wine drinkers think that there are two types of wine: red and white. Or dry and sweet. Or affordable and otherwise. So it is with beer. Some beerdrinkers believe that there are two kinds of beer: Canadian and imported. Or pricy and very pricy. Or advertised and not. Or what they've tried and what they haven't. Or bottled and draught. Like wine connoisseurs, beer lovers need to go beyond these either-or pairings, and develop a sense of style.

As with wine, some beer styles are subsets of a major style. In addition, styles tend to intergrade; they are not always discrete, but tend to blur at the edges of an adjacent style. It is therefore debatable how many distinct styles of beer exist. It's fair to say that there are at least twenty distinct beer styles, and perhaps closer to thirty.

To begin, ale and lager are two very useful tags, partly because they are zymurgically precise, and because they divide the beer family into two large clans.

An **ale** is usually—not always and everywhere—a beer fermented with *Saccharomyces cerevesiae*, the traditional ale yeast that acts best at temperatures in the 15-20 degree Celsius range. Ales are called "top fermenting" because the yeast tends to collect near the top of the fermenting beer before it falls to the bottom of the fermenting vessel. The fast, warm fermentation of ales often imparts a full, faintly fruity flavour.

A **lager** is a beer fermented at colder temperatures, roughly 10-15 degrees Celsius, using *Saccharomyces cerevesiae uvarum* (or *carlsbergensis*), the traditional yeast for lagers. This cool fermentation is often followed by a cold (0-4 degree) aging-conditioning period. Lager is a newer style of beer than ale: in the millenniums-old history of beer, lager was born yesterday. Until the late 19th century, almost all beer brewed commercially was ale. In Germany, the term for traditional, top-fermenting beer is *alt*, which means "old," i.e., ale, the old beer style. Lagers are "bottom-fermenting" beers in that the yeast tends to work at the bottom of the fermenting vessel as it converts the sugary wort into alcohol. Lagers are generally "hoppier" than ales in taste (although they may use less hops in the brewing process), and often "cleaner" tasting, due to their cool fermentation and cold conditioning.

As we have noted, lager production has gained and continues to gain at the expense of ales worldwide.

While this description makes beer sound like a binary possibility—either ale, or lager—the world of beer is much more complex than this split might seem to suggest. Beer style and flavour depend, of course, on ingredients. And much also depends on three important non-ingredient variables: the strain of yeast used, mashing and fermenting temperatures, and brewing method.

In Ontario the difficulty of describing style is compounded by the similarity of mainstream ales and lagers. While beer style is critical for beer connoisseurs and quality brewers, style is practically irrelevant for most of the bland beer brewed by Canada's big brewers. The better and the more interesting the beer, the more important style characteristics become.

To further complicate things, beer styles evolve. While the major Canadian contribution to the world's beer styles —the "Canadian ale style"—has been degraded in recent times by the large brewers (diminishing use of malt, increasing use of adjunct, blandification), we believe that Ontario may yet make contributions to beer style. Quality lagers now being brewed in Ontario (e.g., Creemore, Brick Premium, Upper Canada, Sleeman) suggest the possibility of an Ontario lager style evolving. Algonquin's fruity Special Reserve, Niagara's malty Gritstone, Hart's fresh Amber, Conners' straight-ahead Ale, and Wellington's traditional but wonderfully complex ales suggest many possible Ontario ale style contributions.

The following taxonomy is not comprehensive. It represents only a few beer styles: those brewed in Ontario, and those useful for Ontario beerdrinkers to know about. It should be noted that by volume sold and consumed, over 90% of the beer brewed in Ontario would fall into the "international lager style" or the "Canadian ale derivative" style. These are mere ancestral ghosts of what were once honest, full-flavour styles.

Ales

Canadian ale: Does this style still exist? Until the late 1960s, many would have said that Molson Export and

Molson Stock examplified a distinct style of ale—the "Canadian ale" style. The moderately bitter, husky-rough characteristic of this style was largely the result of using six-row barley (less delicate, more "husky," than the two-row variety commonly used in Europe), as well as limited corn adjunct, which, in quantities of up to 20 or 25% probably didn't diminish the malt flavour in the final product. Now, higher levels of adjunct and lower levels of bitterness from less assertive hopping make most former examples of a Canadian ale style bland and middle-of-the-road. The style, perhaps best exemplified by Molson Stock ale, should probably now be thought of as "Canadian ale derivative."

Pale ale: Classic pale ales have roots in the Burton-on-Trent region of England with its hard water containing calcium sulfate and carbonate minerals. Now the term refers to a variety of ales ranging in colour from straw to deep amber. Pale ales need not be pale. Pale ales should be fruity, a characteristic which is sadly diminished in recent years (Algonquin Special Reserve is a wonderfully fruity beer), or "rounded" (e.g., Wellington's SPA). Pale ales are medium-bodied, low-to-medium in maltiness, and well bittered.

India pale ale: India pale ales were brewed for the long sea voyage from England to India and thus were highly hopped and more alcoholic than a standard ale to help preserve their "shelf life." The heavy hopping means that the aroma is flowery and full. Because the original gravity (see Glossary of Beer and Brewing Terminology, Appendix B) should be quite high, e.g. 1060-1075, and the brew highly hopped, Labatt's IPA cannot be considered a true example of the style. The taste of an India pale ale should be bitter (40-80 International Bitterness Units: see Glossary, Appendix B, "bitterness units"), with medium maltiness.

Strong ale: Deep copper to amber in colour, strong ales are defined in this guide as having 6% alcohol by volume or more. Strong ales are medium-to full-bodied, and have a malty, sometimes fruity sweetness with a medium to high level of bitterness for balance. The antecedents of the

Ontario strong ale style are from Britain: India pale ales, "extra special" bitters, and "barley wines." The high level of alcohol means that strong ales tend to need relatively long conditioning. Niagara Falls' Old Jack and Wellington County's Iron Duke are examples of strong ales.

Bitter: The most common form of beer sold in Britain, virtually always on tap. The fact that bitter is a draught beer is critical to the British who value bitter's low carbonation and lack of pasteurization. Beer similar to a bitter, but sold in a bottle, is usually called pale ale. Bitters are usually bitter in taste from the generous use of "bittering" hops, but are sometimes marked by detectable malt-sweetness as well. While hop bitterness is detectable in the flavour, seldom are hops noticeable in the aroma. Bitters range widely in flavour and strength, with original gravities (see glossary) ranging from 1036 to 1055. In Britain, bitter is often categorized and priced by strength. "Ordinary" bitter (1036-1042) is lowest in price and strength; "special" bitter (1043-1049) is stronger and pricier; "extra special" bitter (1050+) is the strongest and dearest. Wellington's Arkell Best Bitter and Conners' Best Bitter exemplify the style.

Wheat beer: Another beer family. Also known by the German tags "weissbier" (a sour style from the north of Germany) and "weizenbier" (a spicy, clovelike style from Bavaria) and the Belgian "witbier" (or "blanche" or "white"), wheat beer is an intriguing beer style. Anywhere from 30-60% wheat is used to supplement barley as a fermentable. Confusingly, wheat beers can be either ales (top-fermenting) or lagers (bottom-fermenting). German wheat beers have a tart fruitiness and acidity that makes them thirst-quenching and suitable for hot summer days. Some German wheat beers are quite low in alcohol, e.g., 3% alcohol by volume, making them even more attractive as a summer drink. The acidic flavour sometimes suggests lemon, sometimes grapefruit, sometimes cloves and sometimes apple. Wheat beers are not highly bitter: usually from 10-20 International Bitterness Units. Wheat beer can be served with a slice of lemon, or mixed with a cordial such as raspberry. Upper Canada's Wheat is a good introduction to the style, and Ontario brewpubs are increasingly brewing summer wheat beers.

Porter: cola-coloured (dark brown to black) from the use of black malt, and sometimes hinting at a coffee or burnt-toast flavour from the use of roasted barley, porter owes its name to the bag carriers of nineteenth century London who favoured this full-flavoured drink. In addition to pale and black malt, licorice and even molasses can be employed. Porters have less "mouth feel" and body than stouts, but are similar to stouts in some respects. They have a strong, distinctive flavour. Medium to heavy bittering hops balance what might otherwise be a cloying flavour. Bitterness levels of 30-55 International Bitterness Units are common. The best examples come from outside Ontario: Catamount's Porter from Vermont and Cock o' the Rock Porter from Big Rock Brewery in Calgary. We predict that Labatt, which brews Velvet Cream Porter, will soon face porter competition from Ontario microbreweries.

Stout: known to most Ontarians through exposure to the classic Irish dry stout, Guinness, stout is in itself a family of beer. The dry Irish style is one side of the family; there is also an English, somewhat sweeter style, although dry stouts are also made in England. Another stout style is the **Imperial Stout** style, which should have a high original gravity (at least 1070) and high alcohol content (usually over 7% alcohol by volume) for longevity when exported. Roasted, unmalted barley gives stouts their characteristic dark bitterness. Flaked barley is also often used. Bitterness levels in stouts can be quite high. According to Fred Eckhardt, Guinness Extra Stout sold in the U.S. has 50 International Bitterness Units, while the "same" beer sold in Ireland has 90 IBUs!

Cream ale: A confusing term. Cream ale usually refers to an American ale/lager hybrid, in which case ale is blended with lager, the lager usually forming the bulk of the beer. The roots of this style may come from the last century when, in an effort to gain marketshare, North American brewers tried to make lighter tasting, less full-bodied beer than the full-flavoured ales and lagers then on the market. Cream ale can also refer to an ale which undergoes the additional cold-temperature conditioning associated with lagers. Sleeman's Cream ale is not a lager-ale hybrid; it is all ale.

"Real ale": not a style so much as an article of faith for many beer enthusiasts. Real ale is any kind of ale that is neither filtered nor pasteurized (pasteurization literally kills beer) *and* that is "cask conditioned." The result is a beer different in kind—a quantum leap away—from its pasteurized, artificially carbonated counterpart. To make a real ale, the brewer must put the beer into a cask at the end of its primary, or most vigorous, fermentation. The beer, with yeast still active, is "conditioned" as it undergoes a gentle secondary fermentation in the cask. This conditioning produces a delicate, natural carbonation. The result is a startlingly different, fresh and seductive flavour. Real ale is by definition a draught-only beer. It has a short life-span (no more than a few days once the cask is tapped) and it changes in flavour and character during this life-span. Because real ale is fragile and demands knowledgeable bar staff to keep and serve it, real ale is not as widespread as it should be. Wellington County Brewery was the first brewery in recent times to produce real ale in Canada.

Lagers

Ontario lager: no such style yet exists. The promising lagers made by Upper Canada, Brick, Sleeman and Creemore suggest that an Ontario lager style may be evolving, featuring a straw colour, hoppy nose, light malt and medium bitter palate, and a hoppy-dry finish.

Bock: Bock is often a seasonal beer, appearing at Christmas and in the springtime. In Europe, Bock is strong: more than 6.5% alcohol by volume. The aroma should have a pronounced, even intense, maltiness, and the lightly hopped flavour is sweet or semi-sweet and malty. There may be roasty hints of chocolate. The colour varies from dark copper to amber. Brick's Anniversary or Spring Bock is an example.

Pilsner. True Pilsner needn't be brewed in Plzen, Bohemia. But many North American beers that call themselves "pils" or "Pilsner" or "Pilsener" are quite lacking in the essential characteristics of the true pilsner style. Pilsners are pale straw or gold in colour, slightly malty and *very* well hopped. "Well hopped" means two things: bittering hops to produce a level of bitterness quite astounding to some North American palates (often 35-45 International Bitterness Units, three to four times the bitterness of, say, Budweiser), as well as the judicious use of aromatic hops (often of the Saaz or Hallertau variety) to impart a powerful grassy-floral nose. (Appropriately, Plzen means "green meadows.") Flavour should start crisp and bitter with detectable malt, and finish dry and bitter.

Eisbock: an unusual, very strong (can be over 10% alc./vol.) bock by virtue of being frozen one or more times to remove some of the water and thus increase the alcohol concentration. Strong malty nose; intense caramel-malty flavour; sweetish. Amber to mahogany in colour. The intensity of the malt flavour can mask bitterness levels which are technically very high. Niagara Falls Brewing makes an eisbock.

"International lager" style: a very pale (light straw coloured), bland, clean, unremarkable lager with less than 15 International Bitterness Units. Hops not very noticeable in the aroma. Often made with more than 30% rice or corn adjunct.

Light: not a very meaningful term. In Ontario, light tends to mean low in alcohol, and unfortunately, light in flavour and low in interest. Much, but not all, "light" beer is made by adding water to regular beer (as opposed to brewing from a low original gravity). Most "light" beer is "lager," i.e., bottom fermenting. Because light is an ambiguous term, we wish brewers would use more precise style terminology.

Dry: another confusing term. Dry should mean the opposite of sweet; it doesn't or shouldn't mean lacking in flavour or aftertaste. The wave of "dry" beers we've seen in the past few years follow Japanese "progress" in engineering yeast strains that ferment normally unfermentable dextrins. Because more of the beer wort is fermented, fewer "unfermentables" are left. Consequently, flavour is diminished. We say: If you don't like the taste of beer, drink something else. We also say: beers with a short finish (or aftertaste) are fine, but don't call them "dry." People who do are all wet.

A word about ingredients

With the exception of wheat beers, good beer consists largely or exclusively of the three classic Reinheitsgebot ingredients: water, malted barley and hops. Yeast is not really an ingredient but will impart its own characteristics to the beer.

Some of the Ontario brewers draw attention to the **water** they use—"pure spring water" for example—and this is important, for beer is about 95% water. Few brewers detail the more important dissolved minerals. Calcium and sulfate, for example, tend to increase bitterness by enhancing hop bitterness. Sodium and magnesium tend to accentuate beer flavour. Chloride helps to "round out" bitterness. Different waters are therefore suited to different beer styles. In general, hard, carbonate waters (like Guelph's) are most suited to darker ales, while soft water (like most water from inland lakes) can carry soft delicate flavours well.

Malted barley, usually called "**malt**," is the heart of any beer. And the largest part of this heart is a light malt which brewers tend to use as a base, adding darker, more highly roasted malts for colour and more complex flavour. The light malts most commonly used as the base of Ontario beers are two-row and six-row barley malts. Some barley ears have the grain arranged in two rows, and some have it in six. Traditional European malts were almost exclusively two-row, and in the early days, most North American barley was of the six-row variety.

Many brewers regard two-row barley as superior, but some brewers like the huskier, grainier, sharper, less-smooth flavour that comes from six-row, and many brewers use the six-row variety with skill and subtlety. Moreover, Canadian barley growers have increased their ability to grow high-grade two-row barley over recent years. Some skilful brewers like to combine two-and six row malts, Wellington County for example.

Pale malt is the main malt out of which almost all beers are made. In either its two-or six-row guise, pale malt provides the brewer with a foundation on which to build. Brewers add "specialty" malts, darker in colour and resulting in different flavours, to the pale malt base for different effects, but pale malt usually represents more than 80% of the malt used. Six-row pale malt is commonly used in ales and lagers with adjuncts; two-row pale is commonly used in all-malt beers.

Vienna malt is lightly toasted, and thus slightly darker than pale malt. It is used in Dortmund-style lagers and in sweeter Vienna-style beers. Used alone, it produces amber coloured beers.

Carastan covers a range of malts commonly called "crystal" malt in Britain and "caramel" malt in the U.S.A. Carastan is made by drying the malted barley at very high temperatures (up to 100° C.), which helps convert soluble starches into sugars. Depending on roasting temperature and time, colour can range from straw to bronze. Carastan adds sweetness and body to beer, and helps keep a beer's head from dissipating. It also adds colour: a deep copper hue. Carastan is used in a large variety of beers.

Chocolate malt is deep sienna to chocolate in colour. It produces a roasted grain flavour, and is used sparingly in Oktoberfest beers. It is commonly associated with porters, and sometimes stouts and bocks.

Black malt is barley malt so highly roasted that it's

charred. It even smells a little like charcoal. Used primarily for colour—brown to black—black malt also imparts a sharp bitterness that is prized in many stouts and porters.

Roasted barley is *unmalted* barley that has been roasted almost to blackness. It adds a coffeeish note to porters and stouts, but can be used sparingly in lighter coloured ales as well.

Unmalted barley can help produce a creamier head and add a grainy flavour to beer.

Corn and **rice,** two common adjuncts, are often converted to soluble starches before being fermented. Both adjuncts save the brewer money. Both lighten the body and the flavour, rice especially, although corn has its own sweet and maizy flavour which shows when used in high proportions.

Wheat tends to lighten the body of beer and make the head creamy and long-lasting. It can add a "toasty" flavour. Some wheat beers are distinctly lemony, clovelike and/or cinnamony, but this is partly due to the brewing method and the yeast used.

Hops haven't always been part of beer, and beer can be made without them. But hops add so much to beer it's hard to imagine a brewer going without them. Hops add bitterness, thus balancing the sweetness that comes from malts, and contribute greatly to aroma as well, often a grassy, or floral, or haylike bouquet. In addition, hops help head retention and prolong shelf-life. That's right: hops are a natural preservative. Beer is fragile, and generally deteriorates from the moment it's bottled, but hops diminish the rate at which this deterioration occurs. Hops' preservative nature gives them an important role in beers which gain balance and "roundedness" through long conditioning.

Hop cultivation goes back to ancient Greece and Rome, and spread slowly over the centuries, reaching England in the fifteenth and sixteenth centuries where it revolutionized beer taste and beer making. Initially, however, hopped beer was seen in England as a foreign, very Continental threat to traditional unhopped ale. By the mid-sixteenth century, as English brewers recognized hops' ability to inhibit infection of beer (hops retard the growth of some bacteria) and as beerdrinkers grew to like the bitter character of hopped ale, hop use became more acceptable, and hop cultivation spread in the south of England, especially in Kent.

At various points in history, people have made a tea by infusing hop cones in hot water. The result is a medicinal drink with sedative qualities. (Hops are related to marijuana.)

The greatest commercial hop growing centres are Germany, England, Australia, and Washington and Oregon states in the U.S. British Columbia also produces some hops.

Hops and hop extracts can be added at almost any time in the brewing process, from early in the "boil" to just before bottling. The timing is critical to the effect that hops will have on beer. Generally, hops added early in the boil, called "bittering hops," add to the bitterness, but have no great effect on the beer's aroma. The later that hops are added to the other ingredients, the more hoppy the flavour and the more impact on aroma. If hops are added near the end of the boil, they are called "finishing hops" or "aromatic hops." Adding hops late in the brewing process is called "dry hopping" and can produce a marked hoppy aroma.

Hop bitterness is noticed most by the beerdrinker at the back of the tongue.

Yeast is the essential non-ingredient ingredient in beer. Or not in beer: most bottled beer is so tightly filtered that yeast cannot be detected. More a catalyst than an ingredient (it is actually classified as a fungus), yeast is the living micro-organism, the mysterious alchemical agent, at the heart of fermentation. It converts malt's fermentable sugars into alcohol. There are hundreds of strains of yeast used by brewers, each strain having different properties and effects.

How to savour and evaluate beer

It would surprise more than one fraternity boy to be told this: you can significantly *develop* your ability to enjoy beer.

That's right. If you think you enjoy beer now, you can work at (if that's the right term) enjoying it more. This largely involves learning how to savour and evaluate beer. You don't have to turn drinking into a laboratory experience, but you do have to learn the fundamentals of beer style and beer assessment. This learning in turn requires developing a mental template with which you can provide a context for thinking about each beer as well as developing a beer-specific vocabulary to describe beer.

Developing a sense of style requires exposure to a good number of quite different beers. You wouldn't have a very good idea of altbier, or wheatbeer, or bitter, to name but three styles, without having tried at least five brands, and perhaps ten or twenty, within each style. Learning about beer style takes time, and one usually develops knowledge of style, and a beer-specific vocabulary to characterize beer, over a lifetime.

Learning to *evaluate* beer will also help you develop your ability to enjoy beer. Essentially, evaluation consists of paying close sensory attention to several aspects of a beer, attaching words to the sensations, and then placing these sense impressions within the larger context of beer style characteristics. The end result is an evaluation or a rating.

The result may be a rating, but the objective is to deepen your knowledge of and appreciation for, beer.

Note-taking is essential for beer evaluation, and a useful tool even when you are "only" savouring beer. The rating/evaluation sheet (Appendix A) is a good place to take notes. For beer evaluation, it suggests you rate beers out of twenty points, with four for aroma, ten for taste, and six for enjoyment. There are many possible variations, and you may want to devise your own rating system. For beer savouring, disregard the numeric aspect, and take qualitative and descriptive notes.

To evaluate a beer, we suggest something akin to the following procedure. Elements of the procedure may be used informally to savour beer.

Devise a beer grouping. A given beer is best evaluated with at least one other beer to allow comparison. A single beer should be evaluated in a group of similar beers, i.e., beers of the same style. A beer grouping can be two, three or four different labels. Given the volume of beer you have on hand, it's easy to do an evaluation with friends. It's also fun, and discussion helps you develop your beer knowledge.

Examples of beer groupings: 1. Arkell Best Bitter (Wellington County), and Publican's Special Bitter (Upper Canada). 2. Gritstone Premium Ale (Niagara Falls), Upper Canada Dark, Molson Toby. 3. Labatt's Guinness, Pub Draft Guinness (Guinness, imported), Colonial Stout (Upper Canada), and Imperial Stout (Conners). 4. Premium Lager (Brick), Country Lager (Algonquin), Upper Canada Lager, and Premium Lager (Creemore Springs). Other groupings are suggested in the Ratings section of this guide. It's often interesting to put an import or a homebrewed beer into a beer grouping.

Serve the beer properly. If you don't own good beer glasses, buy some. Different beer glass styles have evolved for some of the beer styles, e.g., the "sleeve" for bitter, the tall pilsner glass for some of the lagers, etc.

Drinking beer out of a good glass adds a great deal of pleasure to beerdrinking, and some glasses can add to the sensory impressions made by beer as well. A good start in your beer glass collection would be six to eight clear glass, tulip-shaped glasses. You need clear glass to appreciate a beer's appearance, and a shape that will trap aroma. Use beer glasses for beer only, and wash with plain warm water—no detergent! Milk, coffee, tea and detergent can leave an oily film on glass which will taint the beer. Don't wipe these glasses dry. Allow them to drain and air dry. Some people think you should rinse the glass with cold water just before filling it with beer (to prevent bubbles from clinging to the glass), but we don't think it matters.

All the beers in your beer grouping should be served at the same temperature. If you have a cool cellar, get to know it better—which corners are relatively cool, and which are relatively warm. If you do have a cool, old-fashioned cellar, it will be easy to serve beer at a temperature which enhances the flavour and aroma of the beer. The key to proper temperature is moderation. Good beer should never be refrigerator cold (3-6° C), nor should it be Canadian room temperature (20-21° C). Most lagers should be served 9-12° and most ales 13-14° ("cellar temperature").

Pour three or four ounces (90-120 ml.) into the glass, trying to produce a one-inch head. The head of a beer is important, both for aesthetic reasons and because the head helps prevent oxidation of the beer. (Oxidation is one of the reasons that the last few mouthfuls of a beer drunk slowly can have a metallic bitterness.)

The glass should not be full: you want to leave room for the bouquet.

Listen to the beer. The sound a beer makes as its head collapses can be very useful information to the beer evaluator. Generally—there are many exceptions—the quieter a beer is, the better. A head which collapses quickly and noisily is often the mark of a beer with inadequate malt and hops. ("Head stabilizing" agents are sometimes used by breweries to try to mask this problem.)

Look at the beer carefully. The colour of a beer in different lights is a pleasing aesthetic experience, but don't postpone for too long the next step, smelling the beer.

Lagers often have a pitted or craggy head. Bubbles in the beer and in the head itself should usually be small, often the smaller the better. Copious, large bubbles rising in the beer are often a telltale sign of artificial carbonation.

Note how long it takes for the head to collapse. Almost all beers should have some head left after a minute. Many poor ones don't.

Note also whether there is any "lace" (sometimes called

Belgian lace)—the beautiful and intricate pattern of white head residue—clinging to the sides of the glass when the sample has been drunk. Good lacing can be a strong indicator of the quantity and quality of ingredients in a beer. No lace at all can mean inadequate malt.

Smell the beer more than once. Because the "aromatics" of a beer diminish rapidly, you need to smell the beer quickly after you pour it. It's probably best to do your visual evaluation at the same time as your olfactory (aroma) evaluation. The most common odours in beer bouquets are maltiness (in either a fruity sense or an earthier, grainier sense), and hoppiness, sometimes redolent of hay or grass or meadows. Experts claim that 80% of a beer's flavour can be detected in the aroma, so you can see how important smelling a beer's "nose" is for formal evaluation and for the pleasure of savouring. In a negative sense, faults in the aroma are almost always confirmed in the flavour.

Many bland "international lager" style beers have almost no aroma.

Make notes on sound, appearance and aroma.

Taste the beer "front" to "back." Take a sip and think with your tongue. Using the lexicon that follows, think about the initial impression the beer makes on your tongue. Generally, sweet flavours are most noticeable at the front of the tongue, and bitter flavours at the back.

Try to note *flavour characteristics* more than good/bad, like/dislike. Take another sip, and pay attention to the initial taste before you swallow, as well as any possible differences in flavour after you swallow (the aftertaste, or "finish"). Most beers have an aftertaste which is different, sometimes quite different, from the taste. The aftertaste of a beer is one of its many pleasures, notwithstanding some of the claims made for "dry" beers. (Imagine *boasting*, as the large brewers have, that your beer has no aftertaste! It's like a theologian boasting that his/her religion has no afterlife!) Again, try to attach precise terms to the taste and aftertaste.

Swirl the glass to release the aroma, and smell again.

Take a third sip, swirling it in your mouth, and think about the various flavours in relation to each other. Ask yourself: Are the flavours complementary? Is the overall impression balanced? Before you swallow, breathe in some air: this will boost the impression made on your tongue and your nose. Your sense of taste and smell can diminish, but "resting" your senses for fifteen seconds will help recharge them a little. Make your final notes.

The overall goal of this process is to place the beer in its style context, to describe its unique character, and then, bearing in mind the beer's style, to decide how successful the beer seems to you.

Beer flavour words: A taster's lexicon

While the words used to describe beer can sound a bit like a Monty Python sketch—"a round little number, say twelve, with a phenolic, mildly plastic start sliding to an oaky buttercup finish"—words are the best tool available for learning about beer and beer style, for communicating about beer, and for assessing beer.

Most beer flavours fall into three loose categories: sweet, bitter and sour. Many sweet flavours come from residual malt sugars which have not fully converted to alcohol. Corn adjunct also causes sweetness. Hops boiled with the malt ("bittering" or "boiling" hops) is the major cause of bitterness. Sourness, not often salient in Canadian beers, but common in many Belgian beers (and quite a seductive characteristic it is), can result from the yeast used. It can generally be said that the Belgians value sourness, the British bitterness, and North Americans sweetness.

People are affected by the same beer aromas and flavours in quite different ways. Part of the reason for this is physiological. The tongue is most sensitive for most people just before lunch. Smoking and lack of sleep reduce the ability to detect bitterness. Temperature also affects taste: warmness increases the ability to detect sweetness (and many beers seem to "sweeten up" as they warm). Aging tends to reduce bitterness and increase sweetness in many conditioned beers. Psychological and contextual factors also affect taste.

Your enjoyment of beer will increase as you build your vocabulary for describing it. The flavour words below are some of the most common ones used by beer connoisseurs. We think it most useful to organize the terms into four clusters: sweet, bitter, sour, and a ragbag of terms called "other." Some of the terms occur in more than one cluster. "Fruitiness," for example, is usually a kind of sweetness (and most associated with ales), but is sometimes a good word to describe a kind of low-intensity sourness.

Many of the flavour terms are also used to describe aroma.

Sweet (detected mostly at the tip of the tongue)
- buttery: when pronounced can indicate wild yeast or bacteria
- caramel, butterscotch, toffee
- floral
- fruity, estery: an essential taste characteristic of many ales. Fruitiness may hint at bananas, melons, apples.
- malty
- molasses
- nutty: acorns, hazelnuts, brazilnuts, pecans and walnuts are some of the nutty flavours (and smells) found usually, though not always, in ales.
- sherry, wine, port, vinous

Bitter (detected mostly at the centre-back of the tongue)
- astringent, tannic
- burnt, burnt toast, charcoal
- coffee, espresso
- crisp: fresh, clean, sharp (sometimes more sour than bitter)
- earthy, peaty
- floral
- grainy: like a fresh cereal grain
- grassy, haylike, hoppy: from hops

- metallic: tinny, or sometimes iron-like, usually from hops; undesirable in excess.
- smoky
- sulphury

Sour (detected mostly at the half-way-back edges of the tongue)
- acidic
- citric/lemony
- fruity
- green
- fresh: sometimes yeasty flavour of young or draught beers.
- tart: pleasant clean acidity
- vinous

Other
- alcoholic, warming: hot and, well, alcoholic
- burnt, toasty
- dry: absence of sweetness, as used in the wine lexis. This term has been recently abused by brewers to denote little or no aftertaste. As with a good burgundy, however, dryness in beer can in fact denote strong flavour.
- earthy, peaty
- floral, flowery: usually the mark of Hallertau or Saaz hops
- herbal
- hoppy
- hay, grass: drying hay, often found in well-hopped lagers
- rounded
- salty: rare, but sometimes from water used in brewing
- soft
- smoky
- spicy
- yeasty, breadlike

Off-flavours
- cidery, estery: like apple cider
- corn-like, maizy: the result of too much corn adjunct, often a sweet taste
- paper, cardboard: can indicate a freshness or storage problem. A paper/cardboard odour or taste indicates stale, too-old beer, from too much oxidation or exposure to sunlight or fluorescent light. Warm storage of beer can contribute to cardboard flavours as well. When beer is fresh and well stored, paper/cardboard aroma can also indicate over-use of adjunct, particularly corn.
- vegetal

4
THE RATINGS

The rating scheme explained

Beer ratings sometimes seem to have the veneer of objectivity about them. As if a computer, or robot, had evaluated the beer. Computers and robots do not—and indeed, cannot—evaluate beer, for the whole concept of evaluation exists in a human, cultural context. Sophisticated laboratory equipment can *analyze* beer, and there are even plans to use odour-detecting equipment to minimize problems in the brewing process, but that's another story. Only people can evaluate beer, thank goodness. And beer rating systems are based on the judgment—the personal, subjective judgment—of the people who devise and use them.

Which is the case here. The beer ratings below represent (need we say it) the author's opinion. However, every possible effort was made to rate the beers as fairly as possible. Each beer was evaluated at least twice, and often three or four times. Each beer was tried "blind" at least once, and at least once in a "sighted" tasting. Most of the beers were evaluated in different groupings, e.g., Labatt's Classic was tried in a blind grouping with Creemore Springs and with Niagara Falls Trapper, and then later tried (again, blind) with Brick Premium and Molson Canadian.

Of course you'll disagree with some of the ratings. Good. *De gustibus certe disputandum est!*

Think about your disagreement, and try to put it into words. This will help you develop your beer knowledge. You may find it useful to note comments and your own ratings in the margins of this guide. We hope you'll photocopy the rating/evaluation sheet (Appendix A) and conduct your own evaluations. And of course you'll want to vote in the Beer Ballot (end of chapter six) for the beers you personally rate highly.

Brewpubs have been listed following the ratings, but have not been given star ratings in this first edition of *The Ontario Beer Guide*.

A five-star system has been used to rate the beers. An explanation follows.

★★★★★ A world beater, the best a beer of its style can be: excellence in every technical regard, and a flair for using the *art* of brewing to make the beer unique, interesting and seductive.

★★★★ 1/2 An excellent and exciting beer: much to admire, much to think about, much to enjoy.

★★★★ An excellent, well-crafted beer faithfully representing its style, or pioneering new style properties.

★★★ 1/2 A very good beer.

★★★ A good beer. Good technical properties and honestly brewed, sometimes lacking a little in distinction or interest.

★★ 1/2 A fair beer with no offputting characteristics.

★★ A drinkable beer suffering from either economy of ingredients, short cuts in brewing, or simply lack of distinction or character. May have identifiable flaws.

★ 1/2 A beer drinkable to the thirsty and undemanding beerdrinker ("lawnmower beer"). Often characterized by inadequate barley malt, overgenerous use of corn or other adjunct, and poor carbonation.

★   Poor: cheap, adjunct-laden, sometimes noxious beverage made without the brewer's pride. Lacking discernible malt flavour. A beverage with few characteristics of good beer.

1/2 ★   Awful: a thoroughly noxious drink. Does not deserve the name "beer," but may warrant laboratory analysis.

You'll notice the ratings have much to do with generosity of malt, with character and interest, and with the daring and successful use of the brewer's art and craft. Elevator music may not hurt people, but it doesn't advance the cause of musical beauty, musical creativity, or music appreciation. This is to say, some of the lower ratings indicate blandness as much as badness.

An important point: the ratings are based on world beer standards. The beers evaluated are brewed in the province of Ontario, but we take no provincial approach, i.e., "good for a local beer." A four-star beer, for example, is quite simply an "excellent, well-crafted beer faithfully representing its style, or pioneering new style properties." Not "excellent for Ontario." Excellent period. The best beers in Ontario are as good as the best in the world, as they should be.

Because this guide does not compromise on standards, many of the ratings may seem unduly harsh. They are not. A two-and-a-half-star rating, for example, is neither harsh nor miserly. It designates what we believe to be "a fair beer." Nothing wrong with that. In other words, the rating system has no inflation built into it, and like a non-inflationary economy, it takes some getting used to, but ultimately maintains confidence in the system.

Please note as well that ratings depend very much on style. A given beer is not good, fair or bad in an abstract sense. Beers are brewed to style, which means that you cannot compare Upper Canada Wheat with Hart Amber (a very "green" pale ale with wheat in it, but not a wheat beer) any more than in wine you can compare a German Riesling with a California red. Upper Canada Wheat should be compared with other wheat beers, and Hart Amber should be compared with similar beers (like fresh brewpub pale ales). This is an important point for those who are used to having a (i.e., one) favourite beer, and who forget that each beer is an example of a beer style, and that the style is part of a larger family of beer styles.

In this guide, each beer has been evaluated largely in the context of the style to which it belongs.

The descriptions explained

We have tried to rate each beer brewed in the breweries of Ontario. If we have missed any brands, please let us know.

With the exception of Labatt and Molson, which are listed first, the breweries are listed alphabetically. Brands are also listed alphabetically under the relevant brewery.

We have not included any "near beers" or "non-alcoholic beers" or "de-alcoholized" beers. Arbitrarily we have set the minimum alcohol level at 2.5% alcohol by volume. This level permits the inclusion of traditional, low-alcohol styles as well as the newer "light" beers, but it excludes very low alcohol and no-alcohol malt-based beverages. We have not included malt-based, artificially flavoured "coolers" or shandies.

Each brand has been given a star rating. The alcohol-by-volume is listed. To the extent possible we have also listed the brand's original gravity ("O.G.": see the glossary in Appendix B), as well as the brand's ingredients.

We think it important for beerdrinkers to know the ingredients used to make the beer they drink. People have a right to know the ingredients in every comestible and potable they buy. More important, we believe that having some understanding of beer ingredients makes the beer-drinking public more sophisticated, more interested and more demanding. The more educated the Ontario beer-drinking public becomes, the less likely we are to see the rise of neo-prohibitionism, and the more likely we are to see a flourishing and interesting beer culture. A knowledgeable beer public is therefore good for brewers and good for beer. Listing ingredients is, we believe, in the interest of brewers and the beerdrinking public alike.

The Ontario Beer Guide is the first consumer beer publication in Canada to list ingredients. We hope that soon all brewers list all the ingredients used for a given beer somewhere on the packaging.

The Big Two breweries

Labatt and Molson warrant their own section of the ratings simply because as large commercial breweries, they have much in common with each other, and little in common with small breweries. Much of what we have to say about their beer is critical. The criticism springs from the perspective of this beer guide, the perspective of the knowledgeable and interested beerdrinker.

Because Molson and Labatt have such a long lineup of brands, many drinkers have come to believe that this lineup represents variety in beer. In fact, most of the forty-odd brands sold by the two large brewers are very much alike. An analogy: if the world of beer variety (style and taste) were represented by the length of a yard stick, the variety among Labatt and Molson products would take about one inch. Missing completely are bitters and bocks and doppelbocks, brown ales and old ales, real ales and cream ales, fruit beers and wheat beers, Vienna-style and Dortmund-style lagers, white beers and red beers, etc.

Cynics sometimes say that the Big Two brewers only brew one beer and then put different labels on it. We are not that cynical, but we are impressed with the overwhelming similarity of many of their beers, label to label.

For years Molson and Labatt have been "chasing the centre," and in general, chasing the same market: young, insecure, conformist males who seek group identification. "Smoothness," blandness and sameness are the result for most Big Two brands. Molson used to make a Porter, a characterful and malty beer we thought, but they dropped it. Labatt and Molson have dropped many so-called "marginal" brands, i.e., brands with some identifiable character. Perhaps this is because beers with identifiable character present problems for large brewers: drinkers may pay more attention to the beer than the packaging (!), and then they just might think about and discuss differences among beers (!!). As a result, characterful beers do not lend themselves well to the mindless lifestyle advertisements favoured by the large brewers.

Together, Molson and Labatt have about 95% of the Ontario beer market. We predict that this share will decline over the next four or five years to about 85% as they face more competition from both the low end (Wet Air from the U.S.) and the high end (quality suds, both domestic and imported). Molson and Labatt may also see profit margins eroded. Selling in protected markets has given these two large brewers much larger profit on beer, on a volume basis, than the profit normally gained by large American brewers. Molson and Labatt also spend roughly twice as much money on marketing as U.S. brewers on a per-bottle basis.

Of great concern to the two brewers is the "flat" beer market. Typically, Molson and Labatt blame declines in sales on external factors and bad luck: poor weather, "cross-border shopping," a diet-crazed populace, an aging population, changing values, etc. One wonders when the Big Two will start blaming the alignment of the planets for declining beer sales.

As competition heats up in the 1990s, Molson and Labatt will face serious challenges. We believe that Molson, most especially, is in danger of losing its historic reputation as a quality brewer. Molson was aggressive in the 1980s on the business side, and its mergers and alliances were forward-looking in some respects. On the brewing side, however, its beers seemed to become even more bland and less "beer-like." Its new Amstel is a terrible disappointment. While Labatt has brewed more than a few bland beers, it was the only large Canadian brewer to introduce an all-malt, high quality beer during the 1980s: Labatt Classic, a Reinheitsgebot beer, which, interestingly, is also profitable.

If some of the ratings of Molson's and Labatt's Ontario brands seem harsh, perhaps it's because some of the beers brewed by these two large brewers are poor. Most of the major national brands are pasteurized and have high levels of adjunct.

When beer is regarded not as the world's most heavenly potable—a barley-malt elixir, one of humanity's greatest achievements—but as a manufactured, marketing-driven product, the result is, well, just that: a manufactured product. We hope that in the future Labatt and Molson will make a larger contribution to the Ontario beer renaissance than they do at present.

LABATT BREWERIES
451 Ridout Street North
London N6A 5L5

Labatt is part of the huge Brascan company.

Brascan owns so much of Canada—Noranda, MacMillan Bloedel, Canada Wire and Cable, Royal Lepage, London Life, and Maple Leaf Ogilvie, to mention just a few of Brascan's holdings—that Labatt, in such a business empire, becomes just a box on the "Consumer and Industrial Products" segment of the organization chart. Other boxes in this segment, are, interestingly: The Sports Network, BCL Entertainment (rock concert promotion), Supercorp (69% owned by Labatt, production of TV commercials), Dome Productions and The Toronto Blue Jays (90% owned by Labatt). Other companies related to Labatt are Ault Foods (Sealtest, Light 'n Lively, Balderson cheese) and Johanna Dairies (dairy operations in the U.S.).

Labatt, like some of the large American breweries, has forged links with entertainment-related businesses. Labatt's own advertisements show that Labatt regards beer as a manufactured "entertainment" product, like rock videos. Consequently, we are left with the impression that the actual beer in the bottle is sometimes less important to Labatt than demographics, marketing, and image-building.

Labatt is very packaging-oriented. Changes in bottle design have been touted as major improvements to the beer drinking public. Like its rival Molson, Labatt does a lot of psychological and demographic market research, and then spends huge sums of money targeting the sought-after segment of the population, trying to persuade these people that a given beer is "their" beer. For example, Labatt has recently pushed Budweiser heavily in the Quebec market as the "rock'n' roll" brand, the beer for pop and rock music fans.

About 5% of Labatt's annual production is exported to the United States. Labatt Ontario Breweries is the largest part of Labatt Breweries of Canada. Labatt's largest brands include: Blue, Blue Light, Labatt Extra Dry, Classic and 50, as well as brewed-under-licence Budweiser, Carlsberg and Carlsberg Light.

Labatt lost marketshare following the Molson-Elders merger. It now has about 42% of the national market and roughly the same percentage of the Ontario market. It has about 4,000 employees in eleven breweries, but three or four breweries are likely to close as provincial beer barriers fall. Labatt closed its Waterloo brewery in 1992.

Interestingly, for a brewery best known for its "Blue" lager, Labatt brewed only ale until 1911.

Ingredients. Unfortunately, Labatt will not divulge any detailed ingredient information except to say that Classic and IPA are its only all-malt beers. For its basic malts, Labatt, like most domestic brewers, uses Canadian two-and six-row pale malts. Corn grits and high-maltose corn syrup are the main adjuncts used for most Labatt beers. Budweiser, like its American counterpart, is brewed with rice adjunct.

Blue   ★

5% alc./vol.
O.G.: 1045-46
Ingredients: brewer will not divulge.
Pasteurized.

"Blue" got its name in Manitoba decades ago, where drinkers started to call Labatt's Pilsner Lager by the predominant colour of its label. With about 15% of the national market, this single brand is, for many Canadians, beer.

We don't regard Blue as a true pilsner beer. It would be more accurate to call it an "international lager" style beer. Blue is not 100% malt, nor is it as bitter as pilsners should be (25-40 International Bitterness Units). We would guess Blue to have about 15 IBUs. Blue also lacks the distinctive noble hop aroma characteristic of pilsner-style beers: compare Blue's aroma with Pilsner Urquell's, for example.

To paraphrase Oscar Wilde: To be short on one ingredient may be regarded as misfortune; to be short on two is carelessness.

One of Canada's top-selling and most heavily advertised beers, Blue is a standard example of a "national bland."

Blue Light   ★

4% alc./vol.
Ingredients: brewer will not divulge.
Pasteurized.

When we evaluated Blue Light, four medals appeared on the label. We'd be curious to know what these medals are, and when Blue Light won them. The label also says "light pilsner," but devotees of the true Pilsner style would not recognize this product.

Fizzy, poor heading. Aroma: faintly hoppy, faintly maizy. Taste: adjunct dominated, but at least—in comparison with Molson Light—redolent of hops and imparting a bit of bitterness. Slightly bitter front, small finish.

More like corn husk and carbonated cardboard than beer, but less awful, we think, than Molson Light.

Budweiser   ★ ½

5% alc./vol.
Ingredients: brewer will not divulge.
Pasteurized.

Labatt's version of this widely known beer is quite different from the American version, but in this case, and this case only, we're willing to say that the Canadian version is superior. Not by much, but take what you can get, eh?

Still brewed with rice, and perhaps other adjunct as well, we think there's a bit more flavour in Labatt's Bud than in Anheuser Busch's. More important, the bitterness level of Labatt's Bud seems a tad higher than the low (approximately 12) International Bitterness Units in American Bud (the threshold of detectability is 10-12 IBUs).

This is not to say that Bud is a good beer. Its principle defects are blandness and lack of aroma. All beer should have aroma. Bud is also noticeably thin in body and gassy in its mouthfeel.

Carlsberg   ★★

5% alc./vol.
Ingredients: brewer will not divulge.
Pasteurized.

A recent addition to Labatt's "brewed under licence" stable is Carlsberg which used to be brewed in Ontario by Carling O'Keefe.

Assessment: Okay after a tennis game. A pleasant floral nose promises more than the maizy flavour delivers.

Which is too bad. The Danish original has a lovely hoppy nose and delicate malt flavour not captured in Labatt's version. We think the "licence" of "brewed under licence" implies an obligation to a more faithful rendering of the original.

Carlsberg Light ★★ ½

4% alc./vol.
Ingredients: brewer will not divulge.
Pasteurized.

Assessed as a "light" (which we don't regard as a true beer style), Carlsberg Light fares well. Assessed as a lager, Carlsberg Light would have trouble keeping this rating. The artificial carbonation and gassiness is offputting, but we like the hoppy aroma and the noticeable flavour—primarily bitterness with a slight graininess at the start.

Tasting/evaluation suggestion. With a friend who likes light lagers, compare Carlsberg Light with Upper Canada Natural Light Lager. We liked the Carlsberg better. See if you agree.

Both are 4% beers. Both lace nicely. Both are quiet: pour to produce a one-and-a-half-inch head, and then listen to both beers. Unlike many low-end American "Lite" products, these two lights don't have much snap or pop, just a wee crackle.

While the Carlsberg Light has a lager nose (faintly hoppy with a suggestion of adjunct), the Upper Canada has the characteristic Upper Canada "house nose" (caramelly and sweet, almost Geuze-like), which is intriguing, but perhaps inappropriate for a lager. The taste and the finish of each beer are what the aroma promises: the Carlsberg is pleasantly bitter (well hopped, it would seem) and clean from start to finish, overall a pleasant and (for a Light) assertive enough beer, marred only by its too-thin body. The Upper Canada starts over-sweet, then diminishes to something less sweet, but still not bitter. The Upper Canada is also thin in body, but has a bigger "mouthfeel," with characteristic Upper Canada viscosity.

Carlsberg Light's bitterness makes it go well with sweet and/or oily summer meals: julienne salads, chicken fingers, barbecued ribs, etc.

Classic ★★★

5% alc./vol.
Ingredients: brewer will not divulge, but all malt (no adjunct).
Pasteurized.

Classic is an interesting concept, and a good beer. Interesting as a concept, because it was the first all-malt beer introduced by a large Canadian brewer in quite some time.

Classic is "krausened" or "krausen brewed," which means that some unfermented, sugary wort is added to the young, but almost completely fermented, beer while it is in the conditioning tanks, with the object of starting an additional late and gentle fermentation. Krausening produces a soft, natural, small bubble carbonation.

While the benefits of krausening seem marginal in the first sip of Classic, the flavour of barley is much more apparent than in any other lager brewed by Labatt or Molson.

At second sip, the benefits of krausening and six week's conditioning become more evident. They are tangible in Classic's "smoothness," usually a marketer's synonym for lack of flavour, but used here in a positive sense. The malted grain flavour has been fully incorporated into the mildly bitter profile. The carbonation of Classic is superior to many mainstream lagers, again due to the krausening and long, low-temperature aging: more tiny bubbles, less soda-pop fizziness. With more distinctive hopping, especially late hopping for aroma, Classic would be a world-beating lager indeed.

Tasting/evaluation suggestion. Beers are usually served too cold in Ontario restaurants and bars, and usually it doesn't matter. Classic is worth trying at proper cellar temperature (10-13 degrees Celsius, no colder than 10). Try cellar-temperature Classic in a blind taste test with two other Ontario lagers, Creemore Springs Premium and Niagara Falls Trapper. Make notes on aroma, flavour and finish.

Classic Light ★★ ½

4% alc./vol.
Ingredients: brewer will not divulge.
Pasteurized.

Wee, but pleasant nose: hoppy with a hint of carapils malt. Thin, slightly bitter palate. Good, small-bubble carbonation. Short, pleasant finish. Flawless, but lacking interest.

Classic Limited Edition ★★ ½

5% alc./vol.
Ingredients: brewer will not divulge.
Pasteurized.

Classic Limited Edition is brewed once a year at Christmastime. Nice nose: malty, with a hint of caramel and wildflowers. The all-malt basis of this lager is apparent in its initial impression. We like the mouthfeel, with the small bubble carbonation that comes from long conditioning. Limited Edition is "extra aged," conditioned for four to five months.

Classic Limited Edition lacks excitement, however. Far from bland, and yet lacking distinct character, we think Limited Edition needs a touch more bittering hops and a slightly higher starting gravity.

Crystal ★★ ½

5% alc./vol.
O.G. 1045
Ingredients: brewer will not divulge, but include two-and six-row Canadian malt, and corn grits and syrup as adjunct.
Pasteurized.

Some old Labatt fans speak highly of this lager, and to an extent, we can see why. Straw-coloured Crystal is a soft, balanced lager with enough hops to produce a slightly bitter finish. With more malt and aromatic hops, this beer would be even better.

Tasting/evaluation suggestion. This tasting needn't be blind.

The object is to compare two mainstream beers, Crystal and Molson Golden. They make an instructive contrast. In the greater world of beer, with its extraordinary range in tastes and styles, Crystal and Golden are as alike as two peas in a pod. In the smaller world of mainstream beer, however, where beer is often overwhelmingly similar, Golden, a flag-ship brand, and Crystal, a less-advertised brand, do show some interesting and illuminating differences.

Golden has the better lacing, and this is often the mark of a better beer. But wait.

Labatt's Crystal has a faint nose, but with a trace of hop-piness to tickle the olfactory glands. Molson Golden also has a faint nose, but what is discernible is adjunct, a corny sweetness. These initial hints are confirmed in the taste. Crystal is slightly bitter to start, thin in body, with a hoppy-bitter, slightly metallic finish. Not big in malt, but beer-like. More specifically, Crystal hints at the hoppy bitterness of a German lager. Golden, by contrast, has a sweet start, and a similar, though diminished, finish. In other words, the aroma and the taste tell us that Golden has less barley and more adjunct than Crystal.

Dry Light   ½★

4% alc./vol.
Ingredients: brewer will not divulge.
Pasteurized.

Pfffft. Thin to the point of anorexia. Not dry. Rather wet, like water. Call the beer doctor! This brand needs some malt!

Duffy's   ★★ ½

5.5% alc./vol.
Ingredients: brewer will not divulge.

In addition to pale malt, Duffy's, Labatt's only beer made exclusively for the draught market, seems to have some malt crystal, or carastan, which gives it increased flavour and body. We don't think this an all-malt beer, however. We would guess that corn syrup and/or caramelized sugar has been used.

We like Duffy's on occasion. Its craggy head and good lacing indicate adequate malt; its deep reddish-amber colour suggests a dash of black malt. Malt crystal dominates the taste; Duffy's may be a tad underhopped. We like the low, but adequate, level of carbonation.

Unfortunately, it's often difficult to try Labatt's Duffy's in competition with Molson's draught-only beer, Rickard's Red. Exemplifying the anticompetitive practices in the Ontario beer market, bar owners are often strongly discouraged by sales representatives from one big brewer from featuring draught beer from the other big brewer.

Extra Dry ★

5.5% alc./vol.
Ingredients: brewer will not divulge.
Pasteurized.

"Dry." "Extra Dry." This product's recent name change reminds us of an old line: "I can't recall your name, but your manners are familiar."

"Dry" shouldn't mean flavourless, but, aping the Japanese, Labatt must think it does. See "dry" in the glossary, Appendix B.

Almost no aroma; little taste; a hint of cardboard in the finish.

See also *tasting/evaluation suggestion* under Molson Special Dry.

Extra Stock ★★

6.5% alc./vol.
Ingredients: brewer will not divulge.
Pasteurized.

At 6.5% alcohol by volume, no wonder we can detect a bit of ethyl, as well as hops, in the aroma of Extra Stock.

Introduced to mark the coronation of Queen Elizabeth II in 1952, Extra Stock is Labatt's strong beer, or "malt liquor" as they say. Style? We think this is an ale, but we wouldn't bet the mortgage on it.

With its grainy, slightly thin body, Extra Stock has inadequate "mouthfeel" for a strong ale. Pleasantly bitter finish.

The light straw colour of Extra Stock points to its major defect: the lack of darker malts needed to balance the grainy, thin, ethyl notes. Strong ales are delightful when complex, malty and balanced. The complexity and depth of the flavour should be the reward for—given the extra alcohol—drinking less volume. Extra Stock has 30% more alcohol than regular beer, but its rewards are limited.

50 ★ ½

5% alc./vol.
Ingredients: brewer will not divulge.
Pasteurized.

Introduced to commemorate fifty years of service by "John S." and "Hugh" Labatt, Labatt's 50 was originally known as Labatt's Fiftieth Anniversary Ale, and, in days gone by, nicknamed "Annie."

Fifty is often said to be a sweet ale, but try it side by side with Molson Export, and you won't find it all that much sweeter. This is partly due to decreasing levels of bitterness in Ex over the years.

With a slight, perfumy nose and no discernable malt flavour, 50 is unremarkable. Too much adjunct.

Genuine Draft ★ ½

5% alc./vol.
Ingredients: brewer will not divulge.
Not pasteurized.

When Genuine Draft was introduced in the spring of 1992, it provoked controversy and charges from Molson that the packaging and the label were imitative of a "genuine" (sic) draught beer from Miller, with whom Molson had licensing links.

Except for the name, the beer itself is hardly worthy of controversy. Except for the name? "Genuine Draft." In a bottle yet. And you thought "dry beer" was an oxymoron! You can't get draught beer out of a bottle. Pigs can't fly. Both facts have been known for some time now. If you want flying, go watch birds. And if you want draught, go to your local and ask for it.

At cold temperatures, Genuine Draft is almost devoid of aroma, lacking even a hint of malt or hops. As it warms a little, we notice the slight papery aroma associated with corn adjunct. (This is part of the reason so many mainstream beers are served cold.)

Like many commercial beers, but unlike most real (*really* genuine) draught beer, Genuine Draft is badly over-carbonated.

We like the bitterness of this beer (lager?) both at the front and finish of the taste, but could not detect any malt in the palate, partly as a result of overcarbonation, and partly as a result of overgenerous use of adjunct vis-à-vis malt.

Guinness Extra Stout ★★★

5% alc./vol.
Ingredients: brewer will not divulge.
Pasteurized.

Labatt's version of this world-famous stout was the first beer (1965) to be brewed under licence in Canada.

Stouts should have very stable and quiet heads, and Labatt's Guinness does. Aroma: black malt and roasted barley, balanced and nicely offset with aromatic hops.

Flavour: complexly bitter, enticing notes of burnt grain. Medium-bodied: that is to say, for fans of the original Irish Guinness, this version is sadly thin. Guinness should be full bodied, portly, even fat!

Long aftertaste. Not a bad beer, not bad at all, but when

a beer calls itself Guinness, it has to be rated as Guinness, and this one is not as good as the real McCoy, not by an Irish country mile. This underweight beer could get pushed around on the beach by a stronger stout.

Tasting/evaluation suggestion. Try Labatt's Guinness in a blind tasting with two other Ontario stouts: Wellington Imperial and Upper Canada Colonial. Even blind, you should be able to distinguish them.

Look at the heads: with the lowest alcohol level, Upper Canada's head will likely dissipate most quickly. Guinness has the lightest coloured head. Many beerdrinkers are fascinated by the fact that a black beer can have an almost white head. Wellington and Upper Canada Colonial have café-au-lait-coloured heads.

Smell the bouquets: Upper Canada's is faint, but hoppy; Guinness's is redolent of both black malt and roasted barley; Wellington's is perhaps less complex, most like molasses.

Taste: Upper Canada Colonial is very thin in mouthfeel, neither terribly bitter nor very big. Guinness is complex: initially malty and bitter in balance, but the bitterness grows in the finish, an intriguing and appropriate change. Wellington is the biggest in flavour: a black malt bitterness offset by a slight toffee sweetness which remains constant start to finish.

We like the Wellington stout best, and the Labatt Guinness almost as much. What do you think?

I.P.A. ★★ ½

5% alc./vol.
Ingredients: brewer will not divulge, but all malt (no adjunct).
Pasteurized.

I.P.A., an older but lesser known ale than Labatt's 50, is considered by some beerdrinkers to be Labatt's only ale worth serious consideration.

I.P.A. has a long history at Labatt. John Labatt brewed and sold an India Pale Ale in the late nineteenth century, and, from 1891-1908, won several prizes for it.

A distinct, faintly fruity and husky-grainy aroma hints at the use of six-row barley. I.P.A.'s head vanishes far too quickly and lacing is inadequate.

Interesting palate profile: from a barely-there initial flavour, a nice balance of sweet (front of the tongue) and sour (side of the tongue) flavours gain in intensity, to fade finally to an astringent, husky, faintly bitter finish.

I.P.A. is "all malt," but still lacks depth of character. It needs more malt, and more assertive hopping. Still, we think "I" is quite drinkable, and a better "easy-drinking" ale than many mainstream competitors.

Tasting/evaluation suggestion. Try, side by side, I.P.A. (all malt) and 50 (which has corn adjunct), two Labatt ales. Rate them using the rating/evaluation sheet at the end of this book. Give them your own star ratings.

Lite ★★

4% alc./vol.
Ingredients: brewer will not divulge.
Pasteurized.

Reasonable head, some lacing. The aroma is very mainstream Canadian: hint of hops, hint of malt, adjunct detectable.

With an adequately bitter palate and the taste of corn adjunct not too dominant, Labatt Lite is a drinkable beer. We prefer it slightly to Sleeman's Toronto Light and to Stroh's Light.

Lacking in malt character. Overly carbonated.

Peroni ★ ½

5% alc./vol.
Ingredients: brewer will not divulge.
Pasteurized.

Poor, quickly dissolving head and inadequate lacing.

Sweet, corn-syrup nose. Adequate bitterness in palate. Bland.

Schooner ★

5% alc./vol.
Ingredients: brewer will not divulge.
Pasteurized.

Fizzy. The collapsing head makes enough noise to scare the birds away from the feeder.

Paper-corn aroma. Sweet, thin, maizy palate, with adjunct dominating.

An insult to all sailboats.

Velvet Cream Porter ★

5% alc./vol.
Ingredients: brewer will not divulge.
Pasteurized.

In the first half of this century, porter almost disappeared as a style altogether, at least in the land of its birth, Great Britain. This may account for our foggy notions about what a porter actually is. In Canada and other lands to which it emigrated, porter was saved from oblivion, but there are many differences among the porters currently brewed in Quebec, Ontario, Vermont, Alberta and California.

"Lighter in body and less creamy" than a dry stout (from greater attenuation), "coffeeish and fruity," says Michael Jackson in describing the modern porter. Some would argue that porter needn't be fruity; we like porters on the dry side with hints of burnt toast and espresso. The deep, almost-black brown colour in porters should come from roasted *unmalted* barley.

It may seem odd that Labatt should continue to brew a porter, when so-called marginal brands are not in favour with big brewers. Sadly, although porter as a style has much to recommend it, Velvet Cream is not a good example of the style. The bag carriers of old London, for whom this style is named, would surely seek better brew elsewhere.

Velvet Cream is therefore of little use to beerdrinkers who want to learn about the porter style. Worse, Velvet

Cream won't win any prizes for its technical characteristics, either. For starters, it is oddly short on aroma: how could this possibly be? How could a porter made from a copious supply of well-roasted malts (with a fair whack of hops to balance the caramel-like malts) lack a hefty nose? The answer, we're afraid, is that Velvet Cream lacks adequate malt and hops.

Other signs confirm a paucity of beer's essential ingredients: no lacing, and a surprising thinness of flavour. The thinness, however, may be a blessing: equally prominent in the front of the flavour are corn, cabbage and caramelized sugar. Velvet Cream almost tastes like 50 with a drop of soya sauce. We suspect that for this brand, Labatt gains more dark colour from caramelized sugar than from the use of tasty, dark barley malt.

When will Ontario microbrewers make a porter? The question is of more than academic interest. If Labatt finds it worthwhile to brew a porter, and several out-of-province micros do as well, why not Ontario micros? If micros thrive by finding and filling niches, is this a niche that has been overlooked?

Tasting/evaluation suggestion. Hold a porter evaluation. Unfortunately, it's hard to find porters in Ontario, but this is the province of opportunity. Use your travelling friends to get hold of two or three North American porters, and evaluate them against Velvet Cream. A porter tasting may teach you a little about this superb, dark and bitter style.

One of North America's best porters is brewed in nearby Vermont by the Catamount brewery. Another first-class porter is brewed by the Big Rock Brewery of Calgary. Yet another good one is brewed by Sierra Nevada of California. If you can get hold of any of these porters, do so, and hold a blind tasting using the rating/evaluation sheet in Appendix A.

MOLSON BREWERIES
175 Bloor St. East
Toronto M4W 3S4

Molson is one of the oldest still-in-operation breweries in North America. Like many large brewing companies these days, Molson is a large, diversified, international operation, in which the making of beer seems to end up somewhere between just another "profitable activity" and an "important facet of the company's operations." In other words, the vice presidents don't spend their time worrying about the latest batch of beer.

Started in 1786 by a British immigrant, John Molson, Molson Breweries is now just part (not even the largest part) of "The Molson Companies Limited," with more than 10,000 employees and assets of over $1,000,000,000. The Molson Companies include Beaver Lumber and Lighting Unlimited; Molstar Communications (a sports and entertainment entity which produces some of Hockey Night in Canada and which owns Club de Hockey Canadien Inc.; as well as a large specialty chemical company, Diversey

Corporation, now the largest ($1.2 billion in sales) part of the Molson Companies.

Merging in 1989 with Elders IXL's North American brewing operations (Elders had just become parent company to Carling-O'Keefe in 1987), Molson acquired a slew of licensing agreements: with Bass Charrington to brew Toby; with Miller Brewing to brew Miller High Life and Miller Lite; with Stella Artois of Belgium to brew Stella Artois, which is a major brand in much of Europe. Molson's recent agreement with Heineken, the world's second largest brewery, may be the start of further international links. Molson is now the largest brewer in Ontario and Canada, the sixth largest in North America, and the twentieth largest in the world.

Molson sells more beer in the U.S. than any other off-shore brewery except Heineken. Molson exports represent 19% of the American import market.

Domestically, Molson has 52% of the Canadian market with just nine large breweries. Molson's Canadian has recently become the largest selling beer in Ontario.

As the largest brewer in Ontario, and the major owner of the Brewers Retail monopoly, Molson sometimes seems arrogant and out of touch with its customers. Molson does not allow tours of its breweries. It discourages brewing staff from talking to journalists. It will not discuss its brewing methods or even the style of its beers. When asked whether Molson Light was an ale or a lager, one Molson employee told us that that was a secret! Molson's public relations department will not even say which beers sold in Ontario are brewed in Ontario.

In addition, Molson will not divulge any of the ingredients in any of their beers. Secrets, secrets, secrets.

Amstel ½ ★

5% alc./vol.
Ingredients: brewer will not divulge.
Pasteurized.

The brewing of Amstel under licence from Heineken Brouwerijen of Holland links Molson with the world's second largest brewery. Sadly, this wretched beer will not make Heineken proud of this link. This is clearly a case in which one wonders what the licence is for, when a beer is "brewed under licence."

Molson Amstel is a betrayal of the fans of the older, pre-Molson Amstel. Until 1991, Amstel was brewed by the Amstel Brewery (Canada) in Hamilton, and it was a three-star beer: adequate malt, noticeable hop bitterness—a quite acceptable version of the "international lager" style. It had flavour, if not a great deal of character, and excellent technical properties.

We tried Amstel Amstel and Molson Amstel side by side in two taste tests, and never have we seen such a vast difference between two theoretically identical beers. We were shocked by the noisily dissolving head and the strong adjunct taste of the Molson product in comparison with the quiet, stable head and the clean maltiness of the older version. There were other differences, as well, all of them favouring the old Amstel Amstel.

Molson hopes that Amstel will be a pioneer in the coming interprovincial beer trade. That is, Molson hopes to sell this Etobicoke-brewed beer in other provinces as the interprovincial trade walls start to come down. Given the taste of this product, we hope this doesn't give Ontario a bad reputation.

Amstel is named after the river in Amsterdam. Does Molson think that the beer should taste like the river?

Black Label ★

5% alc./vol.
Ingredients: brewer will not divulge.
Pasteurized.

Here's a challenge worth pursuing for the fleet of neck. Pour this product into a lager glass to produce a one-inch head, and listen, quickly, to the sound of the dissolving head. You're going to have to be fast: the head dissolves faster than a speeding bullet (well, maybe almost as fast). If you're fast enough, what you'll hear is the static on a cheap radio, the sound of a low-malt, high-adjunct, poorly hopped beer, unable to keep its head even for a minute.

Very faint aroma, hint of corn. Bland taste, with a hint of huskiness and just a smidgen of bitterness.

We remember this beer in the sixties; we thought it was better then.

Brador ★ ½

6.2% alc./vol.
Ingredients: brewer will not divulge.
Pasteurized.

Like Labatt's Extra Stock, this "malt liquor" is pale straw in colour, and in need of more malt crystal as well as some darker malts. We think it needs more hops, both for bitterness and for aroma. In short, this is small beer for a "strong" (ale?) beer.

Faint, slightly fruity aroma. Retains head well. Detectable adjunct on palate. Adequate mouthfeel, but oddly short on malt flavour. Inadequate hop bitterness.

Canadian ★

5% alc./vol.
Ingredients: brewer will not divulge.
Pasteurized.

Knowing that Molson has one of the largest advertising budgets in the country, you may smile when you read the label. We firmly agree with the notion that "An honest brew makes its own friends," but we're not sure why Molson would place this statement on the label of such a heavily advertised beer. Ah well, we've all pretended to virtue.

Before you imbibe: regard the huge bubbles and the rapidly dissolving soda-pop head; inhale, and notice the faint papery aroma. Such an aroma and oversized bubbles often indicate that a beer is far removed from the world of quality Reinheitsgebot beer.

Slight maizy taste. Overall, we describe Canadian oxymoronically: extremely insipid.

Canadian is the largest selling beer in Ontario. Evidently, advertising works.

Canadian Light ½ ★

4% alc./vol.
Ingredients: brewer will not divulge.
Pasteurized.

What little taste there is, is awful. Perhaps the Reverend William Archibald Spooner was referring to the drinking of Canadian Light when he told a student: "You have deliberately tasted two worms and you can leave now by the town drain."

Coors ½ ★

5% alc./vol.
Ingredients: brewer will not divulge.
Pasteurized.

Coors is an interesting, uh, beverage. We don't think that it tastes much like beer.

Sweet aroma. Very sweet, adjuncty palate with no detectable hops or malt. We think this version is noticeably sweeter than the American original (which we dislike for different reasons). It was on trying this beer that King Henry IV was provoked to say: "Loathe the taste of sweetness, whereof a little more than a little is by much too much."

Fizzy mouthfeel, like sodapop. We think Coors is worse than pap; we find it offensive.

Coors Light ★ ½

4% alc./vol.
Ingredients: brewer will not divulge.
Pasteurized.

Less flavourful than Coors, Coors Light is also less offensive.

Export ★ ½

5% alc./vol.
Ingredients: brewer will not divulge.
Pasteurized.

Here is an ale that has gone downhill noticeably in the past few decades, and even, alas, in the past few years. In the 1950s, when "Ex" was still a representative "Canadian ale" style beer, it had a *lot* more bitterness (perhaps twice as much) and, we think, a lot less corn. While Ex used to be more bitter than most Ontario ales, it has become rather sweet of late. And Ex now has a strange aroma, not at all suggestive of hops or malt.

Perhaps the most interesting thing about Ex is that the sailing ship on the label looks like an armadillo when turned on its side.

Tasting/evaluation suggestion. An interesting blind tasting. Chill two beers, Ex and Northern Ale, to about 8-9 degrees C. (slightly warmer than fridge temperature). For this blind test, have a friend pour the two beers into identical, spotless glasses to produce decent one-inch-plus heads. Look, listen, smell, taste: the beers are quite similar.

Similar heads; both leave some lacing. Listen and you can tell, by the absence of a loud fizzing, that both maintain a decent head. Similar-sized bubbles rise in the glass.

Neither beer has an attractive nose. Which one seems sweeter to you? Does one seem corn-vegetal?

As to taste, both seem to us almost identical at 9°: sweet, maizy, and bland, with a fizzy mouthfeel.

Wait ten minutes, and do the rest of this tasting sighted. At a slightly higher temperature a few differences come out, particularly in the taste and aftertaste. While neither beer could be described as winsome, we think the slightly greater bitterness of the Export makes it more palatable (and makes us long for the much greater bitterness of the old Ex). What do you think?

Fosters Lager ★ ½

5% alc./vol.
Ingredients: brewer will not divulge.
Pasteurized.

At cold temperatures, bland. At proper serving temperature, a bit like a soda pop made from canned corn.

Fosters Light ★ ½

4% alc./vol.
Ingredients: brewer will not divulge.
Pasteurized.

Papery nose hinting at corn. Sweet (for a lager) palate.

This rather insipid beer still manages to beat Molson Canadian Light in a blind taste test.

Golden ★ ½

5% alc./vol.
Ingredients: brewer will not divulge.
Pasteurized.

Better than some mainstream "international-style" lagers, but typifying the generous use of adjunct, Golden is one of Molson's best known lagers.

Good lacing. Faint nose. Sweet start. Unremarkable finish. Bland.

Kirin and **Kirin Dry:**
apparently not brewed in Ontario

Lowenbrau ★★

5% alc./vol.
Ingredients: brewer will not divulge.
Pasteurized.

Another "brewed under licence," Lowenbrau doesn't closely resemble the original European lager, which is a light-bodied version of a pilsner. Brewed-in-Munich Lowenbrau is itself a fairly bland lager, but Molson's is noticeably blander. The recently abandoned label had eight medals on it, but we wonder when and where Molson Lowenbrau won them. Might this be the beer version of a false resume?

The Germans should learn that when they lend their name to a beer which is brewed under the Reinheitsgebot at home, but badly brewed abroad, the image of the original product will suffer.

Aroma: delicate, pleasant, and hoppy. The taste is sadly lacking in malt, unlike German Lowenbrau, which has a mildly bitter, all-malt flavour.

Miller Genuine Draft:
apparently not brewed in Ontario.

Miller Hi Life ★★

5% alc./vol.
Ingredients: brewer will not divulge.
Pasteurized.

Unexciting, bland, and in need of hops, but inoffensive.

Miller Lite ★

4% alc./vol.
Ingredients: brewer will not divulge.
Pasteurized.

Our acquaintance with Miller Lite was made, inappropriately, in a fine Toronto bar.

William Least Heat Moon, author of *Blue Highways*, said "drinking light in a fine bar is like watching donkeyball in Wrigley Field." Mr. Moon is, of course, right.

Unpleasant aroma. Fizzy. Maizy taste.

Molson Light ½ ★

4% alc./vol.
Ingredients: brewer will not divulge.
Pasteurized.

We're not sure what "heart" they were referring to in the old advertising slogan "Molson Light has got heart!" This is a heartless beer, but not, alas, characterless. This beer is ghastly.

Tasting/evaluation suggestion. A sighted taste test. For people who like to drink less alcohol, "light" beers are a welcome addition. Here's a chance to compare two: Molson Light and Algonquin Light, both with 4% alcohol by volume.

If the beers are in your refrigerator, let them sit, capped, at room temperature for half an hour. You want them to be served at 12-14 degrees C. Into two identical wide-mouthed glasses, pour each beer to achieve a one-or two-inch head.

To start: listen. Put your ear close to the head of each beer, first the Algonquin, then the Molson. Two completely different sounds. The sound of the Algonquin—tk...tk...tk—is like a gentle rain on an awning, the sound of a good head dissipating. The sound of the Molson Light—crklcrklcrkl—is like tissue paper being crumpled, the sound of a poorly carbonated head in its death throes.

Smell: both have faint aromas, but they're different. The Algonquin has some hops as well as the faint suggestion of adjunct. The Molson smells as if a non-beer-drinking accountant designed it: sweet, vegetal, strangely unlike beer.

Taste: Molson Light (it gets worse) is sweet and cardboardy—a pejorative word in the beer world. The mouthfeel of the Molson is very much like sodapop: fizzy. Together, the fizziness and the sweetness might make some

European beerdrinkers gag. The Algonquin taste is not exactly rich, but it is beerlike with a slightly bitter finish. Not a big beer, but drinkable. Molson's finish is even worse than the start, a vegetal, wet cardboard taste.

O'Keefe Ale ½ ★

5% alc./vol.
Ingredients: brewer will not divulge.
Pasteurized.

Although some old-timers say that O'Keefe was once a good example of the "Canadian ale" style, we think it now a wretched, adjunct-laden product quite dissimilar to quality, all-malt ale. It would be interesting to have a written record of the ingredient list for O'Keefe as it is brewed now, and as it was in the 1950s.

A gassy, corn-tasting beer with no malt flavour and an unpleasant sulphury aftertaste. Little aroma, which, given the taste, may be a blessing.

O'Keefe Ale is the acme of lousy beer. We prefer Brantford tap water.

Tasting/evaluation suggestion. Into two tulip-shaped glasses, pour O'Keefe Ale, and any Reinheitsgebot ale. Close your eyes, and have a friend hand you the two glasses. Breathe in the bouquets. It is unlikely that the O'Keefe will impart much aroma, while the other ale will have an easily noticed malty and perhaps hoppy smell. It's spooky. After you dispose of the O'Keefe, notice the glass. We wouldn't be surprised if there were no lace (see glossary). Lack of lace is often the sign of a poor quality ale.

Old Vienna ★★

5% alc./vol.
Ingredients: brewer will not divulge.
Pasteurized.

Many Canadians, including regular O.V. drinkers, might be surprised to know that there is a real, distinctive style of lager called the Vienna style. True Vienna style beers are copper to reddish-amber in colour (from a reddish-brown malt). They are sweeter and have a maltier profile than most European lagers. While Vienna-style lagers are less common now in Europe, they seem to be undergoing a new vogue in the U.S. We think Wellington County's Lager suggests aspects of the Vienna style.

O.V. may have once been a beer in the Vienna style, but no longer. Grassy nose. Dry, almost woody palate. Thin, bitter finish. These three characteristics point to a beer whose parts don't add up to a balanced whole.

Rickard's Red ★★

5% alc./vol.

Ingredients: brewer will not divulge.

Try to imagine this. You work for a brewery not usually associated with the making of flavourful beer, and you've started to notice that flavourful beer is gaining more and more of the market, especially the draught market. So, you decide to introduce a flavourful draught beer and—we know this is hard to believe—you *hide* the fact that you made it!

Sound impossible? This appears to be the case with Rickard's Red.

We were puzzled by Rickard's provenance the first few times we had it, and thought it a drinkable, if sugary, draught beer. When we asked who brewed Rickard's Red, we were consistently told something like: "Oh, it's some microbrewery somewhere in British Columbia. Some small brewery somewhere in the interior of B.C." Once we were told, "Some old guy brews it. An independent, a real maverick brewer!" We were intrigued.

Then we heard that this was deliberate marketing misinformation. And we read that Molson had decided that fewer pub-goers would buy this new draught-only product if they knew that Molson had brewed it! As *The Financial Post* put it, "Molson hopes to lure beer drinkers with Rickard's Red. A key part of its marketing strategy is to disguise it as a micro/import product so consumers have no idea the beer is made by Molson."

Now you know why you won't see the word Molson on draught handles or on beer mats or posters. For a company that spends tens of millions of dollars on advertising, we find Molson's new-found self-effacement rather refreshing.

Special ★

3.3% alc./vol.
Ingredients: brewer will not divulge.
Pasteurized.

"Not much taste" said one imbiber at our local, trying Special for the first time. "Sort of watery," said another.

"We think every beer should be special. But it's just not that easy because when you lower the alcohol you end up compromising the taste," proclaimed the newspaper ads launching Molson Special.

We don't agree. Over-use of adjunct "compromises" taste more than low alcohol does. There are dozens, if not hundreds, of German, Belgian and British beers that are low in alcohol, but, with dark malts employed judicially, bursting with flavour. A "beer with a taste full of real body and soul," continued the newspaper ad. Egad: who writes this stuff?

The dark straw colour of Special suggests the use of a wee tad of dark malt, perhaps black malt. The head is noisy and short lasting.

We do like the delicate, but welcoming aroma: detectable malt (malt crystal we would guess) and detectable aromatic hops.

Flavour: an earthy, almost smoky palate, is completely overwhelmed by the overly gassy carbonation. Thin, almost watery body. Sharp, tinny finish. We can't tell if this brand is top-fermented or bottom, and there are no style hints on the label.

Special Dry ★ ½

5% alc./vol.

Ingredients: brewer will not divulge.

Pasteurized.

Tasting/evaluation suggestion. We like this beer (marginally) more than Labatt Extra Dry, but less than Brick's Amber Dry. We don't think any of these beers are particularly wonderful, nor even particularly dry. Try them in a blind test and see what you think.

Have a friend pour the three beers into identical tulip glasses and serve blind. Listen: two of the beers sound like newspapers being crumpled. One doesn't. This same beer has the most durable head. This same beer also has the most malt in the aroma.

The "same beer" is Brick's. We find the aroma of Molson Special Dry and Labatt Extra Dry almost so faint as to avoid detection, but with the Molson slightly green and fresh, and the Labatt slightly papery.

Taste: We find the Molson ever so slightly bitter, then ever so slightly sweet. We detect no taste worth thinking about in the Labatt product. We think the Brick is slightly malty.

In a marketer's lexicon, "dry" is supposed to mean almost no finish (though why people would pay good money to avoid aftertaste in a beverage they theoretically enjoy is an interesting question). We don't find any of these beers completely dry. The finish of the Molson is more "neutral" (between sweet and bitter) than dry; the Labatt has a cardboard finish with a hint of bitterness; the Brick has a slightly bitter finish which fades quickly. That is, the finish of the Brick is close to what marketers call "dry," but interestingly, the Brick has the most flavour.

Overall, the Molson Special Dry, and the Labatt Extra Dry in particular, illustrate the hazard of reducing taste to the almost undetectable level: the danger is that what little flavour remains will be noticed, and if it is adjuncty and pasteurized, this is what will stand out.

Stock Ale ★★

5% alc./vol.
Ingredients: brewer will not divulge.
Pasteurized.

More bitter than Ex, and, we would guess, more highly hopped, Stock Ale is largely unremarkable save for good lacing which indicates more barley than other Molson beers. Good mouthfeel, small bubbles.

The glass is half empty: Stock Ale, the "original Blue," was a much more characteristic beer a number of years ago in our opinion: a little bitter, almost smoky, husky, and noticeably malty. In other words, a good example of the "Canadian ale" style.

The glass is half full: Even in its seemingly diminished modern form, Stock is maltier, less adjunct-laden and more bitter than many other popular beers.

Stella Artois ★ ½

5% alc./vol.
Ingredients: brewer will not divulge.
Pasteurized.

In Europe, Stella Artois is a widely available mainstream lager. It is made by one of the largest Belgian breweries. The European version is a light-bodied example of the pilsner style. The Molson version is not completely dissimilar to the European original, but strikes us as blander, the effect, we would guess, of adjunct.

The least amount of adjunct can mask the delicate barley flavour of a true pilsner, and Molson's Stella Artois seems to have suffered this fate. The result is drinkable, but hardly stellar.

Toby ★★★
5% alc./vol.
Ingredients: brewer will not divulge.
Pasteurized.

An amber-coloured, brewed-under-licence ale. We have never tried the British original on which Molson Toby is modeled.

Good, craggy head. Good lacing. Quiet.

Aroma: rounded, malty, hinting-at-hops. Flavour: more bitter than the rounded aroma would suggest—more than 20 bitterness units, we estimate. A note of ale fruitiness shines through the right-on-the-money hop bitterness. We would guess that Toby has a touch of black or chocolate malt. Finish: long and bitter. Overly carbonated, but well balanced. The palate is marred somewhat by the deadness, the cotton mouthfeel, that comes from pasteurization. For this reason Toby on tap should be superior, but we like the bottled version because adjunct is less noticeable.

Tasting/evaluation suggestion. Compare Molson Toby with Beaver Valley Amber, contract brewed by Upper Canada. Use the rating/evaluation sheet (Appendix A) to compare these two vaguely similar pale ales.

Good in barbecue sauce, Toby also goes well with casseroles, ribs and beef.

Trilight ½ ★
2.5% alc./vol.
Ingredients: brewer will not divulge.
Pasteurized.

There are much more sensible ways to reduce alcohol consumption. You can drink less often. You can drink smaller volumes. But as Charles Dickens said, "Drink fair, wotever you do!"

What this offensive "product" will save on your liver will be lost in the cost to your mouth.

They say that John A. MacDonald once said to a temperance supporter, "Please move a little further away from me sir. Your breath smells of water!" We think it likely that the reeking man actually had Trilight on his breath.

BRICK BREWING CO.
181 King St. South
Waterloo N2J 1P7

Predictably, a twin city whose original names, Berlin and Waterloo, allude to two of the great brewing nations of the world is going to have its own beer history and beer culture. Kitchener-Waterloo touts itself as the site of the largest Oktoberfest in the world outside Germany. And indeed, beer roots here owe much to the twin cities' large German population.

The Brick Brewing Company is one of the oldest of Ontario's operating microbreweries. Brewing since late 1984, it is also a fairly large microbrewery with a present annual capacity of 42,000 hectolitres, soon to be expanded. Brick has a Reinheitsgebot orientation, and its approach to beer is similar to many contemporary German breweries.

For the beer tourist, the plant itself is worth a visit. Brick has handsomely restored the (brick, of course) Victorian building in which it brews.

Brick was the first Ontario microbrewery to go public in an equity sense. Shares have been listed on the Toronto

Stock Exchange since 1986, and Brick has recently become profitable.

In 1990, Brick won two gold medals in the Monde Selection competition in Luxembourg. One medal was for Premium Lager; the other was for Red Baron. Then again, in 1991, Brick won gold or "grand gold" medals for its Premium, Red Baron, Anniversary Bock, and Amber Dry beers.

Brick is a specialty brewer in that it brews lagers only, and has a fairly focused product line. Brick has recently furthered its lager orientation and its German flavour by forging links to the Henninger Brau AG brewery of Frankfurt. Kaiser Pilsner is Brick's first beer made as a result of this link.

Tours: Tuesdays, Wednesdays, Thursdays. Please give two weeks' notice.

Amber Dry ★★

5.5% alc.

O.G.: 1050

Ingredients: Canadian two-row and carastan malts; about 15% flaked corn; Hallertau and Yakima Cluster hops.

Slight, malty aroma. Frothy head. Amber Dry is not terribly dry, at least in the sense of no-lingering-aftertaste, and this we consider fortunate. Amber Dry has a lightly bitter aftertaste. Unfortunately neither malt nor hops speak loud enough to give this beer much character.

Style? "Amber" doesn't tell us much. Why do brewers use it? "Dry" doesn't accurately characterize this beer either. Because Amber Dry's colour comes from carastan, as opposed to black malt, and because it has a slightly higher-than-average 1050 original gravity, we think this beer vaguely suggests Marzenbier, the German beer style which is brewed in the Spring (March) for consumption in the fall. Amber Dry, however, is lighter-bodied and flavoured than a true Marzenbier.

We like Amber Dry better on tap, where it has a much

fuller, fresher flavour. See *tasting/evaluation suggestion*, under Molson Special Dry.

Anniversary Bock; Spring Bock ★★★★★

6.5% alc./vol.
O.G.: 1054
Reinheitsgebot.
Ingredients: Canadian two-row, carastan, and roasted barley malts, black malt extract; Hallertau and Yakima Cluster hops.
Not pasteurized.

Drinking bock used to be a rite of spring for many Ontarians. Now, alas, few beerdrinkers in this province are exposed to the strong, complex malt intensity which characterizes a good bock. If Anniversary/Spring Bock were more widely available, we believe a new generation of beerdrinkers would quickly learn the joys of the bock style. In brewing this finely crafted dark lager, Brick has given us an exciting drink, perfect for sipping as the snow falls (or melts) outside.

Brick brews the same high-gravity beer under two labels. Anniversary is a Christmas bock; Spring is a vernal bock. Given the quality of this beer, the double release is doubly good news.

Amber-brown-teak in colour, with a unique sherry-molasses nose, Anniversary/Spring Bock has a creamy-rich malty start, with a noticeable hop bitterness in the (long) finish. Lots to think about. This is bock as bock should be.

Part of the complexity and depth of flavour is the result of using a variety of specialty malts in addition to the pale Canadian two-row: carastan (in generous proportion, we would guess), black malt, and roasted barley. Three months of aging (four-five times the aging time of many beers) help to round the full, almost treacly, malt flavour and take away any rough edges.

This beer is a marvel. While Brick's bocks vary a little year to year, a good year can produce the richest, most interesting bock in North America.

Try with a curry or a tandoori meal. Great with almost any full-flavour food. Great by itself.

Tasting/evaluation suggestion. Serve a Brick Bock and an Upper Canada True Bock at an identical (13 degree C.) temperature, and in identical fluted glasses. Here are two fine flavourful bocks. Both are 6.5% alc./vol. (actually low by international standards; most German bocks are more than 6.8% alc./vol.). Both display excellent lacing: note the head residue on the glass as the beer goes down. You will not find such fine Belgian lace in many beers.

Where you'll notice the largest difference—and this is instructive—is in the nose and the finish.

First, however, notice the head. The Brick bock has a yellowish head compared to the cream colour of the True Bock.

Then, really pay attention to the aroma. Swirl each beer and think about its nose. You may find the True Bock more malty, almost toffee-like. The Brick bock has a more complex nose: molasses-sherry, complex and compelling, almost chewable.

When you drink these two beers, you'll notice similarities in the early flavour, but in the aftertaste you'll notice a big difference. The aftertaste, or finish, of True Bock is short, and quite similar to its start. Brick's bock has a long finish. While its initial flavour is a creamy-rich malty one, it has a bitter-earthy-oaky finish (partly the result of its roasted barley) that makes each mouthful provocative: a doppel experience.

Henninger Kaiser Pilsner ★★★ ½

5% alc./vol.
O.G.: 1047
Reinheitsgebot.
Ingredients: Canadian two-row malt; Hallertau and Yakima Cluster hops.
Not pasteurized.

The first spinoff from Brick's links with Henninger was this splendid straw-coloured lager introduced in early 1992. If this is the future of brewing-under-licence, we are in luck. Brick has made a lager of which Henninger should be proud. Kaiser Pils is a good example of soft-malty German pilsners.

Delicate, subtle, and very, very smooth, Kaiser Pilsner shows brilliantly what can be done using all pale malt, and following Reinheitsgebot requirements.

Light hop aroma. Initial taste impression is of a highly attenuated and clean, but softly malty palate. Hop bitterness rapidly asserts itself, though this is not a highly bitter lager. The finish is mildly bitter and very, very soft—almost too soft. We are very impressed with the level of carbonation. Just right. As the oh-so-tiny bubbles burst on your tongue and massage your palate, you may remember why you dislike the fizziness of so much mainstream beer, "sodabeer" we sometimes call it.

Can a lager be too refined, too smooth? Maybe not.

Premium Lager ★★★★

5% alc./vol.
O.G. 1047
Reinheitsgebot.
Ingredients: Canadian two-row malt; Hallertau and Yakima Cluster hops.
Not pasteurized.

Is an Ontario lager style evolving? Much more flavourful and respectful of ingredient and method than "product" made by the big brewers, yet not aiming to be as sassy as the lagers of Bavaria, Brick Premium is a good example of an honest, unpasteurized all-malt lager. It is most similar in style, we think, to the premium pilsners of north Germany and Holland.

In the aroma, the hops are far more noticeable than they are in most Canadian lagers. We suspect this is due to the generous use of high-quality Hallertau hops with their grassy, fresh aroma. The green and hoppy nose, together with Premium's copper colour, promises to deliver a lot more than a Bud or a Corona. And indeed it does.

Starting with a bitterness and quite subdued maltiness, evolving into something resembling freshmown hay mid-palate, and finishing with a nicely rounded aftertaste, Premium is a treat to drink. Part of Premium's glory is its bitterness. With 26 International Bitterness Units, Premium Lager is twice as bitter as many mainstream lagers (over the years, many mainstream lagers have decreased their bitterness to the scarcely-noticeable 10-15 level), though still less than the 35-40 level of many German pilsners. Some might find Brick just a teensy bit thin, but we think it a very fine lager indeed.

Tasting/evaluation suggestion: Do a blind tasting of Brick Premium, Algonquin Country Lager, and Upper Canada Lager, three Ontario microbrewery lagers.

Which beer has the biggest aroma? We think Brick does, by virtue of more aggressive hopping. Notice that the taste of the Brick Premium is similar to its finish—a soft-malt, gently bitter flavour—while the Upper Canada and the Algonquin diminish in bitterness and gain in sweetness from start to finish.

Brick Premium is a superb accompaniment to hamburgers, salads, steaks, and pita bread sandwiches. Also, a superb beer to have on its own after an afternoon of outdoor work.

Brick Red Baron ★★

5% alc./vol.

O.G.: 1047

Ingredients: Canadian two-row malt; approximately 20% flaked corn; Hallertau and Yakima Cluster hops.

Not pasteurized.

Any resemblance of this beer to Brick Premium is not accidental: Red Baron is a similar beer in terms of ingredients except that it uses corn as an adjunct (and is therefore not Reinheitsgebot), and is less hopped than Brick Premium. The reduced hopping lowers its bitterness to 15 Bitterness Units.

We have sometimes found Red Baron to be less than fresh when sold. When this is the case, Red Baron has a papery nose and a cardboard finish.

When fresh, this lager has a green, almost woody aroma (the Cluster hops), and a sweet palate with corn adjunct noticeable, and a slightly sweet finish. Too gassy for our taste.

Drinking Red Baron side by side with Brick Premium is a good way to learn how corn adjunct affects beer aroma and taste.

CONNERS BREWERY
227 Bunting Road, Unit J
St. Catherines L2M 3Y2

There is life after death, and we are delighted.

Conners, the phoenix of Ontario brewers, is back in business with a new management team. When the original Conners company ran into trouble with overhasty expansion in the late 1980s, Marc Bedard, a financial analyst with a career change in the back of his mind, saw the bankruptcy notice in the newspaper. He called his friend Glen Dalzell, a businessman with a sales, business analysis and marketing background. These two men and their enthusiasm were the impetus for the rebirth of Conners Brewery.

Conners is now brewing in St. Catherines in what used to be the Sculler brewery. The old Conners beers had a good reputation among discerning beerdrinkers, and to capitalize on this loyalty, the new management team deemed it wise to rehire the old brewmaster, Doug Morrow.

"We're not trying to compete with Blue or Canadian," Glen Dalzell, president of the new Conners, has said. For this, Ontario beerdrinkers should be grateful. Conners is indeed geared to relatively small scale, high-quality brewing.

Conners has an all-ale product line, with a bitter, an ale and a stout, and most recently, a "Special Draft."

Tours are available. Book ahead.

Ale ★★★★

5% alc./vol.

O.G.: 1054-55

Ingredients: Canadian two-row, carastan and black malts; brewer will not divulge hops.

Not pasteurized.

This very drinkable amber-coloured ale is complex and thought-provoking. We are fascinated by Conner's use of black malt, not always found in pale ales. Conners must use this specialty malt very sparingly, just enough to provide colour and a hint, we think, of non-hop bitterness.

Quiet, durable head. Before you drink, take a good long whiff: bitter, malty, peaty, and a *soupçon* of butterscotch—a subtle and complex aroma.

Flavour: earthy, grainy and bitter, with black malt dominating the carastan. Just a touch of delectable sourness in the middle. The finish is long, and evolves a little to allow toffee notes to mix with the bitterness. At 23-24 bitterness units, Conners Ale is more bitter than most mainstream ales.

Not soft or "rounded," Conners Ale is distinctive, enticing and very nicely balanced.

I'll BUY THAT

- WAY TASTY

VERY FULL DARK FLAVOUR/AROMA

Best Bitter ★★★ ½   *REAL NICE*

5% alc./vol.
O.G.: 1054-55
Ingredients: Canadian two-row and carastan malts; brewer will not divulge hops.
Not pasteurized.

It can be difficult to make a straightahead, true-to-style bitter with adequate flavour, good balance and some mouth-feel. Conners succeeds very well in doing just that with its Best Bitter.

This is a relatively simple beer whose merits are largely the result of the beer not being pasteurized, of short conditioning (we believe), of the simplicity of malt use (only two malts); and of the quantity or the timing of the hops used.

Dark-straw or light amber in colour. Sweet, malty, rounded aroma, with a hint of fruit (plums?) and flowers. Soft malty palate, lightly bitter. As a bitter, could perhaps do with more than the present level of 18 Bitterness Units to balance the generous carastan use. The finish is similar to the start, but slightly earthy.

Try this bitter with a ploughman's lunch, with tourtiere or with casserole. Or all by itself at your neighbourhood pub.

Imperial Stout ★★★★

5% alc./vol.
O.G.: 1059-60
Ingredients: Canadian two-row, carastan, and black malts; unmalted roasted barley; brewer will not divulge hops.
Not pasteurized.

Misnamed, but not mismade, Imperial Stout is a very fine example of a dry and bitter (but not "imperial") stout. To qualify as "imperial," a stout should be very high gravity (more than 1070) and over 6 or even 7% alcohol by volume. As dry as this wonderful stout is, the peaty-smoky older version was even drier. The Sahara of stouts, we called it.

For those who only know Guinness, Upper Canada, or Wellington stouts as points of comparison, Conners' Imperial requires new bearings.

Start with the aroma: an enticing, strong roasted barley bouquet (hints of espresso, perhaps, or burnt toast), and a summery hint of hops. Wonderful.

The taste of this stout is much the same as the aroma, dominated by the dark, astringent, coffeeish flavour of roasted barley and black malt. You can taste Imperial Stout mostly between the front of the tongue (which detects sweetness) and the back (which detects bitterness). We also detect some sourness, which we like, and don't remember in the old version.

Finish: long, bitter, almost metallic—absolutely appropriate. Imperial's dryness and bitterness make it less cloying than many stouts. Overall, we find this stout deeply satisfying, a real tribute to the style.

An excellent accompaniment to roast pork, wild rice casseroles and barbecued ribs, Imperial is also great with more delicate dishes like souffles. We also drink Imperial to celebrate.

Special Draft ★★ ½

5% alc./vol.

O.G.: 1050-51

Ingredients: Canadian two-row and black malts; brewer will not divulge hops.

Not pasteurized.

Another "draught" that isn't, Conners' Special Draft may best be thought of as a young and simple pale ale. The fact that this Special is an ale as opposed to a lager makes it different from many bottled "draughts."

With its fresh, green and yeasty aroma and its fresh, tart, slightly sharp and yeasty palate, Special Draft actually reminds us of draught beer! Special Draft is also draught-like in its finish: a slight increase in lingering bitterness.

CREEMORE SPRINGS BREWERY
Box 369, 139 Mill Street
Creemore L0M 1G0

Torontonians may think of Creemore as north. Actually it's in the centre. Located in a village south of Collingwood (just up the escarpment), and even closer to, but still south of Stayner (which itself is the town in the recent film *South of Wawa*), Creemore Springs sells much of its beer in the Deep South of Toronto. We wish it were more widely available.

Creemore Springs is an interesting brewery. Brewing only one lager beer, but with a not insignificant 13,000 hectolitre-per-year capacity, Creemore can obviously focus a lot of attention on its one brand, and attain a certain economy of scale. This philosophy has paid off for Creemore. The brewery is profitable and has maintained a high level of consistency in its beer.

Creemore uses spring water, and is a Reinheitsgebot brewery.

Tours by appointment.

Creemore Springs Premium Lager ★★★★ ½

5% alc./vol.
O.G.: 1047
Reinheitsgebot.
Ingredients: Canadian two-and six-row, British carastan and American Carapils malts; Saaz hops.
Not pasteurized.

Creemore Springs is a wonderful beer. A really wonderful beer. A subtle beer to make you contemplate and wonder. And to drink.

Creemore Springs is also one of the best beers in Ontario to listen to and to smell.

Let's start right at the beginning. Creemore's label suggests a 6-7 degree serving temperature. We suggest a little warmer: at least 9 degrees.

Pour the beer to produce a head two or three fingers high, and then listen. Here is one of the quietest lagers you'll ever drive, as quiet as a Rolls Royce. (For contrast, listen to a freshly poured Black Label, for instance. You'll hear a Lada, missing its muffler, as the head noisily dissolves.) Creemore's quietness is a mark of its quality.

Smell: at cool temperatures, Creemore Springs has a faintly malty, faintly haylike bouquet. We like the more intense aroma of this lager as it warms, where the Saaz hops show nicely.

Taste: wonderful balance, wonderful progression. First a soft maltiness, then a soft bitterness (bitterness level of 20 1/2 International Bitterness Units), then fade ever so slowly. Creemore's body is surprisingly big for a beer this gentle in palate. Both the body and the velvet gentleness are aided by Creemore's perfect carbonation. No big gassy bubbles here. Which brings us back to the head, and Creemore's quietness. We think we'll have another.

We would prefer Creemore to use refillable bottles, but this is quibbling. We like this divine lager even more on tap.

GREAT LAKES BREWING COMPANY
30 Queen Elizabeth Blvd.
Etobicoke M8Z 1L8

This newly revived brewery was just in the process of setting up as *The Ontario Beer Guide* went to press.

Peter Bulut, owner. Bruce Cornish, brewer.

Tours are encouraged. Book ahead.

Great Lakes Lager too new to rate

5% alc./vol.

O.G.: 1044

Ingredients: Canadian two-row malt; Goldings and Hallertau-Northern Brewer hops.

Not pasteurized.

HART BREWERIES LTD.
175 Industrial Ave.
Carleton Place K7C 3V7

Using much of the brewing hardware of the old Ottawa Valley Brewing company, Hart Breweries is a recent entrant to the Ontario brewing scene. Opened in the fall of 1991, Hart is a 10,000 HL brewery, one of the few in North America to use an open fermentation method.

At present, Hart is the only Ontario brewery east of Toronto. Given its location in Eastern Ontario, it is suitable that for its first beer, Hart should brew an ale.

While Hart expects to concentrate on profitability and to keep an eye on its one flagship brand in its first year or two, contract brewing for restaurants is a possible sideline. In addition, Hart may, in the future, brew a high-gravity winter beer.

Tours are available. Phone in advance.

Hart Amber Ale ★★★ ½   *TASTY*

5% alc.vol.
O.G.: 1052
Ingredients: Canadian two-row, carastan, and chocolate malts; corn syrup and torrefied (roasted) wheat; Tettnanger, Cascade, Hallertau, and Willamette hops;
Not pasteurized.

Hart Amber is a shocking beer, sure to tickle jaded palates. Brewing consultant Alan Pugsley, who formulated this unique ale, should be proud of the result.

Starting with the greenest, most unpasteurized aroma imaginable, followed by a tart, green, bold and yeasty taste, Hart shows its age: a mere nine days old when bottled.

Youth is not always a prized asset in an ale, but in Hart Amber, we see the desirable and positive opposite of what long conditioning (e.g., Britain's Old Peculier, an old ale; Belgium's Rodenbach Grand Cru, a red ale) can accomplish. Hart Amber is a wonderful example of a young pale ale.

The green, malty front fades to a perfectly appropriate, slightly sour and acerbic, mildly bitter finish. Bitterness level: 28 IBUs. The relatively high bitterness level is masked to an extent by tartness.

An empty glass reveals good lacing. On tap, Hart Amber tastes much the same. We hope that this new Eastern Ontario brewery continues to follow its heart, and keeps unchanged the formulation of this unusual pale ale.

LAKEPORT BREWING CORPORATION
201 Burlington Street East
Hamilton L8L 4H2

The well-appointed Amstel Brewery in Hamilton was bought by Bill Sharpe in 1991 when Amstel's parent, Heineken, decided to close the plant and allow Molson to brew Amstel under licence. It was in this large brewery that the Lakeport Brewing Corporation opened in mid-1992.

Bill Sharpe, who has worked for Carling-O'Keefe and Molson, hopes to sell 200,000 hectolitres per year in the first year or two, and then expand further to take advantage of the brewery's 330,000 HL capacity. Lakeport plans to sell in both the domestic market (Ontario, Quebec and perhaps Manitoba) and the American (New York, Illinois and Michigan).

Lakeport's first beer is to be a lager with 80% two-row malt, 20% corn syrup, and three hops.

No beer was available for evaluation when *The Ontario Beer Guide* went to press.

NIAGARA FALLS BREWING COMPANY
6863 Lundy's Lane
Niagara Falls L2G 1V7

Founded in 1989, Niagara Falls Brewing quickly set out to take some brewing chances and add some excitement to the Ontario beer scene.

Niagara Falls is proof that good brewing can come in small packages. With only a million dollars in startup costs, a relatively small 10,000-plus HL capacity, and fewer square feet than the average north-of-Toronto monster house, Niagara Falls has one of the most impressive lineups of beer of any North American brewery: a darker-than-pale ale, a lager, an eisbock, a "strong ale" (a barley wine or winter warmer), and most recently, a stout.

Ambitiously, Niagara is the first North American brewery to make eisbock, a potent form of bock beer which gains its strength and character from freezing the beer, and then removing ice. This unique fortifying process results in a uniquely malty, velvety smooth, dark lager.

In the past, Niagara Falls suffered some of the consistency problems that often take a young brewery a few years to iron out, but of late we have found most of this brewery's beers to be of consistent character and quality.

Ontarians may see the result of further brewing excitement soon. As we go to press, Niagara is working on a new maple-wheat beer. A new Canadian beer style?

Niagara Falls appears to be daring and ambitious, with its ambition oriented to quality and beer interest, rather than just marketshare. Given this admirable orientation, we won't be surprised if Niagara Falls Brewing Company becomes a shrine for beer tourists in coming years.

Tours available: book ahead if possible.

Brock's Extra Stout ★★★

5.8% alc./vol.
O.G.: 1057
Reinheitsgebot.
Ingredients: Canadian two-row, carastan, roasted barley, and chocolate malts, plus unmalted roasted barley; Nugget, Yakima Hallertau, and Northern Brewer hops.
Not pasteurized.

The latest addition to Ontario's stouts, Brock's Extra is so far available only on draught and at the brewery in Niagara Falls.

Aroma: dry and roasty. Taste: the roasted barley and chocolate malts show clearly in Brock's astringent bitterness. Slightly fizzy. Not quite dense or silky enough for our taste.

Finish: very long, with a nice metallic edge. This is a straight, medium-bodied stout, just a little stouter than a portly porter.

Eisbock ★★★★★

8% alc./vol.

O.G.: 1060

Reinheitsgebot.

Ingredients: Canadian two-row, carastan, ground roasted malts (plus one barley malt the brewer will not divulge); Hallertau hops. Not pasteurized.

Eisbock is more than a label. It's actually a style of beer, albeit a fairly rare one.

Icewine is a familiar concept to wine drinkers: you allow grapes to freeze on the vine, and then press the frozen berries for their sweet, acidic and highly concentrated juice, which is then fermented into an exotic (and expensive) wine. Eisbock (Ice Bock) beer is made by freezing the wort (at temperatures as low as -15° C.) and extracting the ice, which is water rather than alcohol. A beer of only medium-high original gravity, i.e., 1060, is thus made more potent.

Niagara Falls is the first brewery in North America to make this Bavarian beer style. We applaud the results. We stand and applaud.

Amber in colour. The aroma is one of the most seductive we know: sweet, but with dark overtones; fruity (plums, dried apricots, and dates); and a bitter-sweet balance with hints of caramel and fruit sourness. Magnificent. Endlessly fascinating.

Taste: starts with a full, strongly malty impression, and then gains in intensity with a warming, ethyl, peaty middle. The long aftertaste is almost like brandy, but without the sharpness. In fact the taste is very, very soft, very rounded and gentle for an 8% beer. Part of this is due to the gorgeous, delicate small bubble carbonation: liquid velvet on the tongue.

At $6.00 for a 750 ml. bottle, this is the perfect beer to call for after a good dinner, either alone, or with fruitcake or pastries. Why don't more restaurants carry high-end beer? One bottle of Eisbock serves 3-6 people. Serve at 12-13 degrees in large brandy snifters or tulip glasses.

Gritstone Premium Ale ★★★★ ½

5.8% alc./vol.   *WONDERFUL*
O.G.: 1057
Reinheitsgebot.
Ingredients: Canadian two-row, carastan, ground roasted malts;
Hallertau hops.
Not pasteurized.

When this ale first appeared a few years ago, we fell in love. We said, where have you been all my life, you beautiful ale. We said, you are the leading edge of an Ontario ale style: intensely malty with bitterness in balance. We said all those things. Then we bought a case a few months later, and it was not nearly as good. We felt betrayed, and we said, what did you do to yourself. And then we fell in love again.

Over the past three years, we fell in and out of love with this distinctive Ontario ale. We are pleased to report that in the past year our affair with Gritstone has been steady and intense.

Amber-russet in colour, and with a malty, subtly hopped nose (you won't find many ales hopped with the Hallertau strain), Gritstone is a joy to behold. At its best, it should hold a head for a minute or two.

The palate is moderately bitter, with some carastan sweetness and some darker flavours from the roasted malts evident. Only the bitterness lingers in the finish. Which is fine by us: it makes us want another. As Joni Mitchell said, I could drink a case of you.

Gritstone's glory is partly due to the brewer's generous use of malt. The 1057 starting gravity (about 20% higher than most ales) gives Gritstone Premium Ale an intensity of flavour not matched by most lower gravity beers. Add enough hops to adequately bitter the dulcet intensity of the malts, and you get a glorious beer.

A glorious beauty of a beer. A superb, style-forging ale. Try this one with stew, chops, or lasagna. Gritstone is also excellent with a sweet dessert like chocolate cheesecake. See if you don't agree.

Old Jack Bitter Strong Ale ★★★ ½

7.2 % alc./vol.
O.G.: 1062
Reinheitsgebot.
Ingredients: Canadian two-row, carastan, chocolate, and ground roasted malts; Nugget and Northern Brewer hops.
Not pasteurized.

When Shakespeare's Henry the Fifth said "I would give all my fame for a pot of ale" he may have had something like Old Jack in mind. Here is a beer for which it is worth sacrificing fame and more than a little money.

Malty, malty, malty start, with a maltily bitter (the effect of roasted malt) finish. Oh, and at over seven per cent alcohol, you may want to drink this one in small measures with a friend, or in the safety of your own home. Remember, what Henry V actually said was "I would give all my fame for a pot of ale, and safety."

Serve cooler than cellar temperature, warmer than refrigerator temperature.

Trapper Premium Quality Lager ★★★

5% alc./vol.
O.G.: 1051
Reinheitsgebot.
Ingredients: Canadian two-row and ground roasted malts; 20-30% corn; Nugget and Hallertau hops.
Not pasteurized.

Trapper has won an award for its label. We find the beer itself variable: often promising, sometimes flawed.

Copper-coloured Trapper sometimes has a fizzy, quickly dissolving head and large bubbles rising from the bottom. When this is the case, corn is detectable in the nose.

At its best, however, Trapper has a complex, intriguing and intense nose: malty-caramel with a hint of charcoal. We like this unique aroma.

With an oaky-earthy-caramel palate—call it funky—and slightly bitter, almost sour finish, Trapper is unlike any lager you'll try. We'd like it even more if it were more consistent, more hoppy, and less maizy.

NORTHERN ALGONQUIN BREWING
Old Brewery Lane
Formosa N0G 1W0

Northern Algonquin is the modern version of an old brewing tradition. Many older Ontarians can remember with affection the old Formosa brewery, as it used to be called, the only non-unionized brewery in the province, and thus the only brewery which remained open during the beer strikes and lock-outs of the 1960s.

During these strikes and lockouts, many thirsty Ontarians gained their first taste of Formosa Club Ale and Formosa Diamond Lager. In 1988 the old Formosa plant was given a $4.5 million dollar refitting and became Northern Algonquin, a new, and quite different brewing company from the old Formosa.

Northern Algonquin is run by ex-Carling O'Keefe people, and, like Upper Canada, Sleeman and Brick, aggressive in outlook. It is one microbrewery that wouldn't mind being macro. With its 70,000 hectolitre capacity, Northern Algonquin is already a fair-sized brewery, and with hopes of selling its beers in western Canada, Algonquin may grow larger yet.

Algonquin is proud of its spring water, which comes from the Detroit aquifer 300 metres below the brewery.

Tours by appointment.

Banks ★

5% alc./vol.

O.G.: 1048

Ingredients: brewer will not divulge.

You can tell this brand is hugely over-carbonated even before you taste it. Listen to the loud th-th-th-ppp when you open the bottle. Pour a glass and notice the quantity and the size of the bubbles rising.

Fair lacing. Sweet papery aroma. Banks is so highly carbonated that it is difficult at first to taste anything other than a fizzy, saccharine sensation. Sweet maizy palate. Cardboard/wood finish lingers on the middle of the tongue.

We're puzzled by this disappointing beer. While the original Banks is popular in parts of the Caribbean, its tropical provenance, we think this version needs more malt. In a hot climate, many beerdrinkers like a well-hopped, bitter profile to refresh. Algonquin Banks is far too soda-like— bubbly and sweet—to refresh on a hot day.

Country Lager ★★

5% alc./vol.

O.G.: 1048

Ingredients: brewer will not divulge.

Not pasteurized.

Country Lager is an unexciting, slightly sweet lager. Algonquin does not fare terribly well in a comparative taste test with some other Ontario microbrewery lagers (see Brick Premium Lager). You can predict some of Algonquin's weakness by using that under-rated beer-judging instrument: your ear.

Pour a glass to produce a head, and then listen. Crackle, fizz, hiss. The head disappears with a noisy farewell, which isn't apt to happen with an all-malt, well-hopped lager. What causes the noisy collapse? Usually, too much adjunct.

The aroma is faint, sweet, and suggestive of corn. Balanced and bland at the start, Country Lager has a husky, maizy, ever-so-slightly sweet finish. Paper-cardboard notes when not absolutely fresh. Underhopped.

Formosa Springs Cold Filtered Draft ★ ½

5% alc./vol.
O.G.: 1048
Ingredients: brewer will not divulge.
Not pasteurized.

Boy, rating beers can be tough. Especially a bottled beer that thinks it's a draught. (For our thoughts on bottled "draught" and the flight capability of pigs, see Labatt's Genuine Draft.)

What can we say about this beer? Well, for starters, bland can be, well, nondescript. Inoffensive even. But beer isn't supposed to be inoffensive. It's supposed to make a statement. For inoffensive, we drink water.

Tasting/evaluation suggestion. Try Formosa Springs Cold Filtered Draft in a tasting with Pacific Real Draft. We think they are eerily similar: noisy head; faintly grassy, maizy nose; vaguely saccharine taste; with a maizy and papery finish.

Sometimes we think we can tell them apart. Sometimes we think we can't.

Formosa Springs Light ★★

4% alc./vol.
O.G.: 1040
Ingredients: brewer will not divulge.
Not pasteurized.

Formosa Springs Light has good technical properties: it has a good head and it laces well.

We like its aroma: delicately grassy and floral. The taste, we think, is too light, so delicate that it challenges the tongue's ability to detect. Malt is barely detectable.

Fine carbonation gives Formosa Springs Light a silky mouthfeel.

Algonquin Light ★ ½

4% alc./vol.
O.G.: 1040
Ingredients: brewer will not divulge.
Not pasteurized.

With a good head and some lacing, Algonquin Light hints at more rewards than some light beers provide.

Faintly hoppy aroma with just a hint of adjunct, unexciting but beerlike flavour, and a trace of bitterness in the finish. Algonquin Light lager hints at some darker grain, but so subtly as to elude description. We wish brewers would use darker grains more generously in their low-alcohol beers: this is one way to gain flavour without much added alcohol.

See *tasting/evaluation suggestion* under Molson Light.

Special Reserve Ale ★★★ ½

5% alc./vol.
O.G.: 1048
Ingredients: brewer will not divulge.
Not pasteurized.

Special Reserve is one of the fruitiest beers on the market, and good on Northern Algonquin for brewing it.

Fruitiness is one of the key defining characteristics for many types of ale, but so many ale makers, in their rush to brew inoffensive, middle-of-the-flavour-circle beers, have all but eliminated fruity accents. With respect to this important ale characteristic, Special Reserve is a wonderful example.

A rich and full nose, but a disappointingly short head. We like the contrast between the start and the finish: an intriguing complementary mix of grain and fruit in the front of the palate, some hoppiness in the mid-palate, and just a hint of peatiness or licorice in the back.

Special Reserve can be even more beguiling on tap, especially when it is really fresh.

A fine accompaniment to shepherd's pie, steak and kidney pie, baked beans. We also like Special Reserve with old cheddar cheese.

NORTHERN BREWERIES LTD.
503 Bay Street P.O. Box 280
Sault Ste. Marie P6A 5L9

Northern Breweries used to be known as Doran's Northern Ontario Breweries, but was bought out by employees in 1977, making Northern the first employee-owned brewery in North America. Some of the brewing equipment is very old.

Northern Breweries' beer sales illustrate an interesting geo-cultural phenomenon in Ontario. Northern's two main breweries in Sudbury and Sault Ste. Marie straddle the "ale-lager line."

Sudbury, closer to ale-drinking Quebec, drinks a lot of ale, and the Northern brewery there brews Northern Ale. The Soo, close to the lager-drinking United States, drinks more lager than ale, and the plant there brews lager exclusively.

This is a northern extension of the old observation that Yonge Street and Highway 11 separated ale-dominant eastern Ontario from lager-dominant western Ontario.

The Sault Ste. Marie plant has a 90,000 HL capacity, and the Sudbury plant almost 150,000 HL. Northern's sales are almost evenly split between packaged beer and draught.

Forty-five minute tours are regularly conducted in July and August from Monday to Thursday of each week. Book ahead. Phone or write to arrange a tour during the rest of the year.

Edelbrau ★★

5% alc./vol.
O.G.: 1044
Ingredients: Canadian two-and six-row malts; about 26% corn grits; B.C. Hallertau, Willamette and Cluster hops.
Pasteurized.

Edelbrau's lightly hopped nose, dense, small-bubble head, and very good lacing would all seem to augur well.

Unfortunately, the palate is marred by too much corny sweetness and too much six-row huskiness for a lager.

Northern Ale ★

5% alc./vol.
O.G.: 1045
Ingredients: Canadian two-and six-row malts; about 20% corn grits; Willamette, B.C. Hallertau, and Cluster hops.
Pasteurized.

Good heading, but little to recommend this pale ale. Pulp and paper nose, sweet corn palate. See *tasting/evaluation suggestion* under Molson Export.

Northern Extra Light ★ ½

2.4% alc./vol.
O.G.: 1023
Ingredients: Canadian two-and six-row malts; corn grits; Willamette, B.C. Hallertau, and Cluster hops.
Pasteurized.

Northern Extra Light is a tenth of a percent below our 2.5%

alcohol-by-volume cutoff for this guide, but what the heck.

Not all brewers brew light beers from a low gravity. Some brewers simply add water to regular beer; some brewers remove alcohol from the beer. Extra Light is brewed like a regular beer, but from a very low original gravity, 1023.

We like the detectable hops in this very-low alcohol beer, but wish it were maltier. Some crystal and dark malt would help.

55 ★ ½

5% alc./vol.

O.G.: 1044

Ingredients: Canadian two-and six-row malts; about 26% corn grits; B.C. Hallertau, Willamette and Cluster hops.

Pasteurized.

"55" was first brewed in 1955 to commemorate the 75th anniversary of the city of Sault Ste. Marie and the 25th anniversary of the Sault international bridge.

The fact that this lager is nicely hopped almost makes up for the lack of malt profile. Unfortunately, corn dominates.

Superior Lager ★★

5% alc./vol.

O.G.: 1044

Ingredients: Canadian two-and six-row malts; about 26% corn grits; B.C. Hallertau, Willamette and Cluster hops.

Pasteurized.

Superior Lager is like many mainstream products, and better than some. This is what many would term "lawnmower beer."

Poor fizzy head, some lace in the glass, and a faint, sweet, almost papery aroma. Big bubbles, often the mark of artificial carbonation.

Some malt and detectable corn in the taste. Thin in body. The finish is short and slightly sweet. Nothing wrong with this beer that more malt and less corn wouldn't cure.

Thunder Bay Lager
not evaluated

5% alc./vol.

O.G.: 1045

Ingredients: Canadian two-and six-row malts; about 26% corn grits;
B.C. Hallertau, Willamette and Cluster hops.

Not available on tap. Thunder Bay Lager is similar in formulation to Superior Lager.

PACIFIC BREWING COMPANY
6 Peacock Bay
St. Catherine's L2M 7N8

Like Guelph, St. Catherine's is now a two-brewery town, with Pacific and Conners operating. The Pacific Brewing Company, formerly Pacific Western Brewing, is owned by International Potter Distilling of Vancouver, and has been in business since 1990. Its British Columbian parent company started in 1957, and is B.C.'s third-largest brewery.

Pacific started operations by building an efficient $5 million plant with an ambitiously large capacity—100,000 hectolitres—but at present is using only a third of this potential. Plans are afoot to brew another beer exclusively for the export market to better utilize capacity.

Pacific Real Draft ★★

5% alc./vol.
O.G.: 1047-48
Ingredients: Canadian six-row malt; about 25% flaked corn; Cluster hops.
Not pasteurized.

Straw-coloured Pacific has fair heading and less than average lacing. Faintly hoppy nose with corn just barely detectable. Small initial impression on the palate, verging on sweet, changing to a slightly maizy, papery finish. Pleasant, viscous mouthfeel.

Better than elevator music, but not quite Vivaldi. Replacing some of the corn with carapils malt, and adding a second hop would add interest to this lager and make the taste of adjunct less noticeable.

We shouldn't have to say it: "real" draught, "genuine" draught—you can't get draught out of a bottle or a can. Draught beer is always served on tap. Pacific seems to think that a beer that is not pasteurized (or "heat pasteurized" as they put it on the label) is draught. Not so. Draught beer is unpasteurized beer, true, but it must also be, by definition, served on draught. It should be fresh from the barrel, fresh from the brewery, and sometimes, when you're lucky, cask-conditioned, like Wellington County and Hart "real ales."

Ironically, Real Draft was a johnny-come-lately to the draught market: only in 1992, more than a year after being sold in cans and bottles, did Real Draft become available as real draught!

See *tasting/evaluation suggestion* under Northern Algonquin: Formosa Springs Cold Filtered Draft.

SLEEMAN BREWING AND MALTING COMPANY
551 Clair Road West
Guelph N1H 6H9

Sleeman, opened in 1988, has a different game plan than some of the Ontario microbreweries. For starters, President John Sleeman makes no bones about competing to gain marketshare at the expense of the Big Two brewers. He'd like to get 2% of the provincial beer market. That's a significant segment, but with more than 1% of the Ontario market already drinking Sleeman, an attainable goal. Sleeman's five-year business plan calls for nationwide distribution. The brewery already sells in Michigan restaurants and bars, and Mr. Sleeman would like to see further American sales.

Second, Sleeman made brewing-under-licence and high levels of capitalization two of its early goals. To this end, Sleeman has an agreement with Stroh's of Detroit. Sleeman brews Stroh's under licence, and Stroh's has a major stake in the $7 million dollar brewery—19%—as does Manulife Financial of Toronto, with 10%.

Third, Sleeman positions itself not as a start-from-scratch brewery, but rather as a revival of an old Guelph brewery, the Silver Creek Brewery in which John Sleeman's grandfather, great-grandfather and great-great-grandfather were involved.

Sleeman has the image of a cottage brewer, while having the financial muscle and marketing savvy of a large brewery (200,000 HL capacity).

Sleeman contract brews Nordik Wolf Light (unavailable in Ontario) for parts of the American market.

Tours are sometimes possible. Phone to see.

Cream Ale   ★★★

5% alc./vol.

O.G: 1050

Ingredients: Canadian two-row and carastan malts; Chinook and Cascade hops; corn grits adjunct.

Pasteurized.

Cream Ale is a distinct style of North American beer, commonly an ale-lager hybrid. But in Sleeman's version, it's not a blend; it's all ale. The result is something akin to a pale ale, but less malty in character.

Copper in colour. Cream Ale has a promising head—dense tiny bubbles forming a craggy, mountainous topography—a sure sign that the brewer has not been stingy with the malt or over-generous with the corn adjunct.

Cream Ale has a faint, pleasant, grassy nose, the smell of west coast hops. Taste: mildly bitter, mildly malty. Corn does not dominate. Has Sleeman recaptured the classic Canadian-ale style profile? A slight increase in almost metallic bitterness in the finish makes it tempting to open another one.

Good with hamburgers, hotdogs, potato salad, tacos. This would be a terrific beer at the ball game. Cream Ale at the SkyDome? How would Labatt, part owners of the Skydome, handle the competition?

Premium Light
not evaluated

4% alc./vol.
New beer: no further details available.

Silver Creek Lager ★★★½

5% alc./vol.
O.G.: 1048
Ingredients: Canadian two-row and carastan malts; Hallertau and Saaz hops; corn grits adjunct.
Pasteurized.

Like Cream Ale, Silver Creek Lager has a dense, frothy, rocky head. The Hallertau and expensive Saaz hops show very clearly in the fresh, new-mown-hay nose. Delightful.

The taste is bitter, very slightly green and well balanced. The finish is crisp, with the bitterness diminished. A very satisfying lager due to adequate malt and superior hopping.

Silver Creek Lager is one of our favourite beers on the beach, at the cottage, or after a tennis game.

Stroh's ★

4.4.% alc./vol.
O.G.: 1044
Ingredients: Canadian two-row and carastan malts; Cascade hops; corn syrup adjunct.
Pasteurized.

Some of Stroh's advertising is as mind-numbingly sexist as one can imagine. We fail to see how scantily clad young women parachuting into a fishermen's campsite with six-packs of Strohs in hand imparts any of the "superior" qualities vaunted on the label. And on examination, we don't find many superior qualities in this lager either.

Overly sweet, cream-of-corn nose. Big bubbles, poor head, no lacing. Sweet maizy start, paper-cardboard finish. Seems to have only a passing acquaintance with barley malt.

Stroh's Light ★ ½

4% alc./vol.
O.G.: 1036
Ingredients: Canadian two-row and carastan malts; Cascade hops; corn syrup adjunct.
Pasteurized.

Stroh's Light heads and laces better than the regular Stroh's. Like so many mainstream beers, it is far too highly carbonated. Noticeable corn in the palate; very thin-bodied; papery finish.

Toronto Light ★ ½

4% alc./vol.
O.G.: 1036
Ingredients: Canadian two-row and carastan malts; Cascade hops; corn syrup adjunct.
Pasteurized.

Similar technical profile to Stroh's Light. Sawdust aroma due to corn syrup. Very highly carbonated. Sweet start; paper-sawdust finish. Very thin-bodied.

Too light: a beer named Toronto needs more darkness, more heft, more swagger.

UPPER CANADA BREWING COMPANY
**2 Atlantic Avenue
Toronto M6K 1X8**

Upper Canada Brewing's relatively long history (founded in 1984) and large size (for a microbrewery), as well as its terrific marketing savvy, have ensured this brewery an important place among the beermakers of Ontario. A focus on quality and a willingness to innovate stylistically have also helped this 40-45,000 hectolitre brewery to maintain this place. We sometimes wonder if a few of the Upper Canada's brands have become less full-bodied of late, but we are impressed overall by Upper Canada's orientation.

Upper Canada was an independent brewery until 1991 when Corby Distillers (52% owned by Hiram Walker-Allied Vintners, which is itself owned by the giant U.K. firm Allied-Lyons PLC) bought a 40% stake in Upper Canada, and the rights to gain further control in the future. This equity acquisition would seem to indicate that some large transnational companies see profitability and growth in quality beer. Upper Canada, Ontario's first microbrewery to have an export orientation, hopes that gaining access to Corby's distribution system in Europe and the U.S. will increase its sales.

At present, Upper Canada has a little more than half a per cent of the Ontario beer market.

Most Upper Canada beers have a "house nose" so distinct that aroma alone can usually pinpoint the brewer. Most Upper Canada brands have a characteristic malty-caramel aroma, which we find appealing and suitable in some brands, and less so in others.

As a largely Reinheitsgebot brewery, Upper Canada was the first North American brewer to have its beers accepted for sale in Germany.

Tours available Monday to Saturday. Call to arrange.

Beaver Valley Amber ★★

(Thornbury Brewing Company)
5% alc./vol.
O.G.: 1046
Reinheitsgebot.
Ingredients: Canadian two-row, carastan and black malts; Challenger hops

"Contract brewing" is more common in the U.S. than in Ontario. With a recipe, a business plan and adequate financing, you can ask a brewery with excess capacity to brew your beer for you. Beaver Valley is contract brewed by Upper Canada for the Thornbury Brewing Company.

The origin of this ale, however, is evident in the aroma: Beaver Valley Amber has some of the characteristic, malty-caramel bouquet that we like in other Upper Canada beers. In Beaver Valley Amber we also detect a hint of sourness.

Noisy head; poor lacing. An earthy-husky (the effect of black malt), mildly bitter front of the palate evolves to a slightly sour, attenuated finish.

We think Beaver Valley thin in body and inadequate in mouthfeel for the profile. We like the huskiness, but the body and mouthfeel disappoint those of us who expect an "amber" to be fairly robust. In other words, the colour seems to be more of a paint job than a function of style.

What is an "amber" anyway? You won't find this style listed among the traditional styles. Literally thousands of quite different ales and lagers are amber-coloured; therefore the term doesn't denote anything very precise. However, the term "amber" is gaining popularity among North American microbrewers who use it in a very loose way to indicate that a beer is somehow different from bland mainstream beer.

The label says "all natural ingredients"; "no preservatives or chemicals." We wish they'd just list the ingredients, especially when, like Beaver Valley, it is Reinheitsgebot. A beer made completely from rice, corn syrup and soya extract—with no barleymalt at all—could still be described as "all natural ingredients." Another quibble: hops are a preservative; therefore the "no preservatives" tag is not fully accurate, but it may make some folks feel good to read it.

Colonial Stout ★★ ½

4.8% alc./vol.
O.G.: 1046
Reinheitsgebot.
Ingredients: Canadian two-row, carastan and black malts; Challenger bittering and finishing hops.
Not pasteurized.

It's possible to make full-flavoured, big-bodied ales which are still low in alcohol. In Britain, mild and brown ale are good examples of flavourful, low-alcohol beer styles.

It may also be possible to brew a full-flavoured, full-bodied *stout* at less than 5% alcohol, but we suspect it's difficult. Is it misguided to try? Or should the brewer aim for a brown ale or porter instead?

This 4.8% alc./vol. offering from Upper Canada is certainly slim, if not skinny, for a stout. Perhaps it really should be called a porter. Stouts, after all, are porters that have put on weight, i.e., they have heft and body. (Stout was originally called "stout porter.")

Some lacing in the glass, but not enough. Colonial fails the "head test" as stouts should not: almost no head after one minute.

Faint, but attractive aroma: black malt, and some hops detectable. Taste: dominated by black malt. Bitter, but not quite bitter enough for the profile. We like the tartness and the balance between hop bitterness and dark malt bitterness. Thin in body and mouthfeel.

With a dash of toasted barley, we think this would be a good porter. But if Colonial wants to be a stout, it will have to gain weight.

Tasting/evaluation suggestion: see Labatt's Guinness.

Dark Ale ★★★½

5% alc./vol.
O.G.: 1048
Reinheitsgebot.
Ingredients: Canadian two-row, British carastan and black malts; Challenger bittering and finishing hops.
Not pasteurized.

The New World Guide to Beer says that Dark Ale "has over the years lost some of its 'pears in cream' character" and we agree, although sometimes we wonder how much anyone remembers further back than last week. We do wonder if Dark Ale is thinner in body than it used to be.

Dark Ale has one of the *nicest* aromas of any Ontario ale. Nice? Is that a technical term? Well, perhaps we mean a fine balance among three discernable elements: the fruitiness that defines many ales, the dry grainy aroma of a well-fermented, all-barley beer, as well as a nuttiness that characterizes many dark ales. The taste follows the aroma, more or less exactly. The aftertaste surprises a little in that it's pleasantly bitter.

Tasting/evaluation suggestion: Here is a good beer to develop an understanding of the effect of temperature on flavour and aroma. At the same sitting, try Dark Ale Number One served at 4-5 degrees (refrigerator temperature), and Dark Ale Number Two at 12-14 degrees (cellar temperature). You'll quickly appreciate why beer enthusiasts dislike good beer served the way it all too often is: cold. The fridge temperature Dark Ale keeps all of the beer's most attractive qualities locked up. Like summer's most interesting flowers, beer needs a little warmth to blossom.

Try Dark Ale with sausages, chicken, chops; it's also good in meat-based soups and stews. We also like Dark Ale after curling or skating.

Lager ★★★

5% alc./vol.
O.G.: 1046
Reinheitsgebot.
Ingredients: Canadian two-row malt; Hallertau Northern Brewer and Hersbrucker hops.
Not pasteurized.

Unusual for a North American lager, the copper-coloured Upper Canada lager has a detectable malt nose which foreshadows the malty, well-aged, complex flavour. We like the maltiness of the bouquet, but we think the caramel, perfumy, almost Geuzy aspect slightly inappropriate for a lager ("Geuze" is an intriguing sour-sweet Belgian beer style).

Lacing is variable, perhaps less lacing now than formerly. Likewise, the beer seems less hoppy than it used to be.

As to style, Upper Canada Lager is a good introduction to what is broadly termed the "continental" style of lager. High protein continental barleys, according to Michael Jackson, make a more rounded, maltier lager than the lighter "maritime" barleys of Denmark and the U.K. The malty flavour and slightly viscous ("sticky") mouthfeel are highly prized by many south-German beerdrinkers. Upper Canada Lager has this malty stickiness, as well as its own slightly drier finish.

Don't drink this lager too cold. A temperature of 10-12 degrees will provide rewards not even hinted at in colder temperatures. Altogether, a good balance of well-attenuated dryness and full malt sweetness.

Accompanies spicy meals, salty hors d'oeuvres, hamburgers, felafels.

Natural Light Lager ★★

4% alc./vol.
O.G.: 1037
Reinheitsgebot.
Ingredients: Canadian two-row malt; Hallertau Northern Brewer and Hersbrucker hops.
Not pasteurized.

One of the very few Reinheitsgebot low-alcohol lagers available, but this one's a disappointment.

Here the characteristic Upper Canada aroma and viscous mouthfeel actually work against the beer. See *tasting/evaluation suggestion* under Labatt's Carlsberg Light.

Publican's Special Bitter ★★★ ½

X-o-LENT

But Not THE Body of WELL ARKELL

4.8% alc./vol.
O.G.: 1046
Reinheitsgebot.
Ingredients: Canadian two-row, carastan, and black malts; Challenger hops.
Not pasteurized.

Few British bitters have the malty-toffee bouquet which is prominent in this bitter. So much the worse for the Brits, some would say.

Publican's colour is on the borderline between copper and amber. Like many British bitters, Publican's has a thin mouthfeel; unlike many bitters, this one is ever so slightly sweet, finishing in a more bitter direction. In this sense, Publican's will not remind you of the dry and bitter British bitters you've had; rather, it may remind you of Young's or Fuller's, or some of the sweeter Yorkshire bitters.

Not terribly hoppy in the nose or the palate, Publican tells the drinker what carastan malt can contribute to flavour (sweetness) and body (lots of "mouthfeel"). Most of the colour here comes from black malt.

Altogether, highly drinkable. We think Publican's is a *much* better accompaniment to Mexican food than the bland "international style" lagers often recommended.

Rebellion malt liquor ★★★★

6.5% alc./vol.
O.G.: 1056
Reinheitsgebot.
Ingredients: Canadian two-row malt; Hallertau Northern Brewer and Hersbrucker hops.
Not pasteurized.

Although the term "malt liquor" is meant to denote above average strength (i.e., more than 5% alc./vol.), the term is an imprecise one in Canada. To say that a beer is merely strong is to say little.

Strong ales and lagers are often the pride of the brewer's art, not because of the alcohol, but because of the complexity that can be achieved from generous malt use and long conditioning. Strong ales and lagers tend to age well.

This copper-coloured lager benefits from its five to six weeks' conditioning time, long enough to permit a third, slow and gentle fermentation to accommodate and soften (but not lose, thank goodness) some of its edges. Rebellion also benefits from generous late hopping, which adds a good deal to aroma, and which helps balance the maltiness of a high-gravity lager.

The nose is fetching: soft and malty, a little like a British "old ale," a little like a bock, plus a hint of muskiness. On the tongue, an unusual blend of complexity, ethyl notes and smooth drinkability.

Strong beers must compensate the drinker (who drinks less) with remarkable flavour and depth. This one certainly does.

Excellent on tap. Be a rebel, Ontario style: serve Rebellion in brandy glasses as an after-dinner drink.

Sichuan Snow Waves ★★

5% alc./vol.
O.G.: 1045
Ingredients: Canadian two-row malt; American rice extract;
Hersbrucker hops.
Not pasteurized.

The "premium brand of the Chengdu Brewery in Sichuan province," Sichuan Snow Waves is the first oriental beer brewed in Ontario. The use of rice as an adjunct which ferments "cleanly" is common in beer brewed in China and Japan, principally to produce a lighter flavour.

Aroma: ricey, flowery. Flavour: slightly astringent. This delicate beer accompanies spicy and non-spicy oriental dishes.

True Bock ★★★ ½   *WONDERFUL STUFF*
(seasonal, Christmas through Spring)

6.5% alc./vol.
O.G.: 1062
Reinheitsgebot.
Ingredients: Canadian two-row, carastan, and black malts; Hallertau
Northern Brewer, and Hallertau Hersbrucker hops.
Not pasteurized.

Don't fill the glass! Pour this bock into a large tulip glass with plenty of room to trap the aroma: with its malty, toffee-like nose, this bock is as much joy to inhale as it is to drink. It's also a feast for the eyes. Hold True Bock up to the light to see rubies glint in mahogany under its cream-coloured head.

Unlike Brick's bocks (see *tasting/evaluation suggestion* under Brick's Anniversary/Spring Bock), the aftertaste of this beer is similar to its start: a well-balanced malty-bitterness.

We like this beer, with its three month's aging, very much. True Bock changes a little from year to year. Sometimes it's very deep and complex, sometimes a little lighter in palate and body. True Bock has more hoppy bitterness in the taste than many bocks.

A beautiful beer with bratwurst, dark meats, and spicy food. Or try this one all by itself on the first day of spring. Or a day you think should be a little more spring-like.

Wheat ★★★ ½

OK STUFF

4.3% alc./vol.
O.G.: 1041
Reinheitsgebot.
Ingredients: Canadian two-row malt and British malted wheat (roughly 50% of each); Hallertau Northern Brewer bittering hops (no finishing hops).
Not pasteurized.

While wheat beer is relatively new to Ontario, the style is sufficiently wide-ranging in Germany that there it has several sub-style variations. Upper Canada's is closest to the common weizenbier (wheat beer) found near Munich.

Wheat beers are typically thought to be lighter in body and more subtle in flavour than pure barleymalt beers. There is some truth to this, though some of the Berliner weisse style wheat beers have a more-than-subtle citric tang to them.

Upper Canada Wheat is a soft, delicate, and teasingly coy beer. The nose is subtly lemony and floral. The taste initially is slightly—perhaps too slightly—sour, with good mouthfeel and small bubble carbonation, and finishes with a pleasant melange of tartness and bitterness.

On occasion, perhaps when the beer is less than fresh, the head disappears too quickly for a wheat beer, and lacing is sometimes inadequate.

Tasting/evaluation suggestion. Using the evaluation sheet provided at the end of this guide, evaluate and compare Upper Canada Wheat with another German wheat beer. "Weizenbiers" such as Bamburger Kaiserdom wheat beer and Franziskaner Weissbier are sometimes available at Vintages. This evaluation comparison is fun to do with friends on a summer evening. We think the Upper Canada Wheat is less sharp, less acid-sour, less dramatic, than many German wheat beers, but still a good introduction to the style. What do you think?

Another suggestion: when wheat beer is on tap at a brewpub (the Rotterdam and the Amsterdam in Toronto often have wheat beers in the summer), compare the fresh-from-the-tap brewpub product with a bottle of Upper Canada Wheat.

Upper Canada Wheat is a good beer to serve with many types of *al fresco* dining: noodles, salads, club sandwiches, etc. Also good with spicy Malaysian and Indonesian food. Wheat beers are thought to be summer beers, and we won't argue, but we have enjoyed Upper Canada Wheat in the winter with a green salad and fresh-from-the-oven bread.

Idea: put an inch of raspberry juice in the bottom of a pilsner glass, and fill it with Upper Canada Wheat. Or try a sliver of lemon on the rim of the glass.

WELLINGTON COUNTY BREWERY
950 Woodlawn Road
Guelph K1K 1B8

Wellington, in business since just 1985, is one of Ontario's oldest microbreweries—an indication of just how young the Ontario beer revolution is.

Wellington has succeeded admirably in an increasingly competitive environment because it seems to have a clear sense of mission: to brew very high quality beer in traditional British styles. Wellington puts its corporate brewing philosophy on every label: "brewed to the highest standards using only selected premium malts and hops. Using traditional methods, without adjuncts, we strive for perfection in quality..."

When Catherine Parr Traill wrote in *The Canadian Female Emigrant's Guide* ('Hints on Canadian Housekeeping') "There is nothing the new settler complains more feeling of, than the want of good beer and ale," she was likely referring to the likes of Wellington's good beer and ale. For Traill was referring to British immigrants and to

British ale, and Wellington is very much a British brewery in inspiration. Very appropriate, we think, given Guelph's British roots.

Some think that Wellington's only weakness is its lack of bottling facilities. Plastic bottles lack aesthetic appeal and tip easily on uneven surfaces, especially when they are almost empty. Perhaps this is not a weakness, however, but rather a sign of intelligent and adaptive packaging. Small brewers have been known to go broke buying and maintaining bottling equipment, which is famous for its finicky-ness. We'd rather have Wellington brewing and profitable with plastic bottles than not brewing at all.

Wellington is one of the crown jewels of Ontario brewers. Generally, each of the six brands it brews is an accurate rendering of its style, and thus useful to beer novices who want to develop an understanding of style.

Most of Wellington's beers are of highly complex formulation: their County Ale, for example, is hopped at various stages with no less than five varieties of hops. Brad Veitch, Wellington's young and capable head brewer, is also adept with some of the specialty malts: black, chocolate, and carastan.

Tours by appointment.

Arkell Best Bitter ★★★★ ½

4% alc./vol.   *Best Beer I ever tasted*
O.G.: 1038
Reinheitsgebot.
Ingredients: Canadian two-and six-row, carastan and chocolate malts; Fuggles, East Kent Goldings, and Goldings hops.
Not pasteurized.

Don't hurry. Take your time with this one.

And as you pour this copper-coloured brew, leave lots of room at the top of the glass to hold the aroma. Much of the pleasure in this bitter is in its aroma: very fresh, almost "green" (fresh and draught-like), *very* hoppy, and somewhat malty. With its pungent and seductive nose, and only four per cent alcohol, Arkell probably has the biggest aroma-to-alcohol ratio in the Ontario beer world. A true olfactory marvel.

Taste: hoppy, grainy, bitter. Just a hint of carastan shining through. Not big bodied, but big on flavour thanks to aggressive hopping. Some folks detect a hint of almonds or pecans in the taste. Do you?

Finish: hoppily bitter, almost snappy, and ever-so-slightly sour. Notice the bitterness lingering at the back of your tongue.

What does all this add up to? A lot, we think. This is probably the biggest, most flavourful 4% beer (20% less alcohol than average) brewed in Ontario. So, dieters and reduced-alcohol imbibers: take your old industrial "Lite" and pour it down the drain. Rush out and buy this extraordinarily flavourful, brilliantly bitter, bitter.

Accompanies cornish pasties, fish and chips, hamburgers, and sunny afternoon picnics.

County Ale ★★★★★

5% alc./vol.
O.G.: 1052
Reinheitsgebot.
Ingredients: Canadian two-and six-row, carastan and chocolate malts; Northern Brewer, Whitbread Goldings, East Kent Goldings, Styrian Goldings, Goldings hops.
Not pasteurized.

One of the very few North American ales available in a "real ale" format, that is to say, unpasteurized, and, far more important, conditioned after primary fermentation in the cask, County Ale was for many of us the first brewed-in-Ontario beer that showed us what a heavenly beverage beer can be. While delightful out of the (one-litre) bottle, amber-coloured County Ale is a must on tap, where the virtues of cask conditioning are dramatically evident.

Here is an aroma to be savoured. If you're at a pub, you might ask for half a pint in a full pint sleeve glass. This will leave lots of room for a full bouquet to develop. We think the aroma very complex: malty, slightly fruity, ever-so-faintly oaky, and with the Goldings hops clearly evident. The seductive aroma foreshadows the complexity and the malt-hop balance that awaits you in the taste.

We think County Ale has one of the best, most savoury palates imaginable: big, very big, but beautifully balanced. A soft malty start, then a full, slightly bitter middle, which dissolves to a surprisingly hoppy finish. The finish of County Ale—long, bitter and beautiful—makes us pause, smile, and crave another sip.

Here too, in County Ale, is carbonation as God meant it to be. Some think "not fizzy" means flat. Not so. Roll this beer over your tongue for the pleasure of having thousands of minute bubbles—the result of natural carbonation—dissolve on your tongue.

Not as fruity as Algonquin's Special Reserve, County Ale still has an ale fruitiness in both the aroma and taste. In the stampede to blandness and so-called dryness, too many ale makers have forgotten that fruitiness can be one of the glorious characteristics of a good ale.

Imperial Stout ★★★ ½

5.5% alc./vol.
O.G.: 1055
Reinheitsgebot.
Ingredients: Canadian two-and six-row, chocolate and black malts; wheat (under 3%); Progress (bittering) and Saaz (finishing) hops.
Not pasteurized.

Like Conners' Imperial Stout, this stout from Wellington is too low in gravity to be an accurate rendition of the true imperial style, but Wellington Imperial nevertheless delivers imperially on two important aspects of any stout: flavour and mouthfeel.

The aroma hints at the flavour and the finish. Together, the black and the chocolate malts produce a rich and rewarding, molasses-like aroma.

Flavour: strong, almost puckering, black-malt bitterness with some pale malt sweetness still apparent. Hints of licorice. Finish: similar, and very, very long.

In short, we like this beer. Wellington stopped brewing this stout for a period. We can be grateful that it is once again available.

Given its viscosity, you may want to serve Imperial Stout one or two degrees cooler than cellar temperature.

A good accompaniment to stews and to meat pies, Imperial Stout also makes a good dessert beer, complementing (don't laugh; just try it) chocolate mousse, chocolate cheesecake, and chocolate covered almonds.

Tasting/evaluation suggestion: see Labatt's Guinness.

Iron Duke ★★★★ ½

6% alc./vol.
O.G.: 1065
Reinheitsgebot.
Ingredients: Canadian two-and six-row, carastan, and black malts; Goldings, East Kent Goldings, Hallertau and Saaz (finishing) hops.
Not pasteurized.

A real *coup de brassage*, this one! Few strong ales anywhere have the malty depth and the perfect hop balance of Iron Duke. Perhaps this is why Iron Duke, Wellington's second-best selling beer, is so highly esteemed by its fans.

At 6 per cent alcohol (actually on the low side for a beer of this flavour and profile!), Iron Duke manifests all the attractions of a good strong ale: intense, almost port-or sherry-like maltiness, muted traces of ripe fruit (peaches? plums?), and a long evolving aftertaste.

Tasting/evaluation suggestion. In a blind taste test, try Niagara Falls' Old Jack Bitter Strong Ale and Wellington County's Iron Duke. (Add Theakston's Old Peculier to the tasting if the LCBO happens to be selling it.) Serve the beers at 13° C. in tulip-shaped glasses (brandy snifters will do in a pinch). Using the taster's lexicon (chapter three), make notes. How would you characterize the difference in aromas? Do you detect any fruit aroma? Which beer is the hoppiest? The sweetest? Old Jack has chocolate malt which produces a nutty, roasted flavour; Iron Duke has black malt which produces a bitter, burnt-toast flavour: can you detect these malts in the flavours? Which beer has the greatest change in flavour from start to finish?

Lager ★★★ ½

4.5% alc./vol.
O.G.: 1045
Reinheitsgebot
Ingredients: Canadian two-and six-row, and carastan malts; Fuggles, Tettnanger, Cascade and Saaz hops.
Not pasteurized.

As the only bottom-fermented beer, this brand is the odd-man-out in the Wellington family.

Dark straw in colour, Wellington Lager has a very malty nose for a lager: caramelly or toffeeish, rounded, and sometimes, we think, hinting at walnut.

The taste is less malty than the aroma: it starts with a gently bittered maltiness (the effect of Fuggles hops, not often used in lagers, may be evident), and finishes with a quiet and appropriate level of bitterness.

The Tettnanger hops, and perhaps even more, the Saaz, give this beer more of a mid-European profile than many Ontario lagers. Its maltiness, gentle sweetness and rusty colour suggest lager styles few Ontarians are exposed to: the true Vienna style and the Munich pale style.

Because Wellington's Lager may confuse lager drinkers used to either blandness on the one hand, or hoppy crispness on the other, perhaps a name change would help to locate this interesting lager within the world of lager style. "Wellington Vienna-style Lager"?

S.P.A ★★★★ ½

4.5% alc./vol.
O.G.: 1045
Reinheitsgebot.
Ingredients: Canadian two-and six-row, carastan and chocolate malts;
Whitbread Goldings, East Kent Goldings, Goldings hops.
Not pasteurized.

To our thinking, one of the most interesting, sophisticated, and drinkable pale ales found anywhere. S.P.A., or Special Pale Ale, hints at the British tradition of having two or three similar pale ales (or bitters) of different strength and cost: "ordinary" pale ale or bitter (under 4% alc./vol.), "special" or "best" pale ale or bitter (4-5% alc./vol.), and sometimes an "extra special" pale ale or bitter (more than 5% alc./vol.).

Copper colour. Fruity-malty nose. Complex and subtle, S.P.A. is less dominated by malt than Arkell Best Bitter, less green and saucy than County Ale. It is brilliantly balanced, with nutty and buttery notes weighed against crisp and grainy notes. One very classy beer.

Try it with Lebanese sandwiches, tacos, tortas, and chicken salads. Also great with steak and baked potatoes.

5
BREWPUBS LISTING

Ontario is rapidly becoming Brewpub Heaven. Ontario has more brewpubs per capita than any province or state. The Toronto area now has enough brewpubs to make possible, with a little help from public transit or taxis, a variety of brewpub crawls. Partly because of the number of interesting brewpubs in Ontario, beerdrinking tourists are increasingly choosing Ontario as a travel destination.

Because the beer they sell is always draught beer—*real genuine* draught beer—brewpubs are always sought out by beer enthusiasts. Freshness, variety, and seasonal styles of beer, food cooked with beer, beer-knowledgeable servers: there are many reasons to frequent brewpubs. Brewpubs are exciting partly because they aim to please in a very local and particular fashion. A brewpub in Ottawa can brew a beer to celebrate Winterlude. A brewpub in Stratford can brew ale styles that Shakespeare might have drunk. If a style of beer is unpopular, it needn't be brewed again. The beers that are brewed in a brewpub depend on the whim and expertise of the brewer, as well as the demands of the clientele and the season.

Evaluating brewpubs, however, presents challenges. For starters, what should be assessed: the ambience, the service, the food, or just the beer itself? We lean to a close focus on the beer, but even then, problems in evaluation arise.

First, the offerings at a brewpub tend to change over the course of a year, as well as over the years. At least they should. With their small capacity, and freedom from bottling and marketing constraints, brewpubs should be able to brew at least a few seasonal beers and to take a few chances in introducing less-well-known styles. Second, even the "same" beer is more apt to change batch to batch in a brewpub than in a brewery. To an extent, this lack of absolute consistency is a virtue in a brewpub. Unfortunately, however, variations in brewpub beer which might excite a regular patron —"Have you tried the *new* batch of Brown Ale at Gamby's? It's unbelievable!"—make it a slippery business for the evaluator.

The next edition of *The Ontario Beer Guide* will give each Ontario brewpub an overall rating (as opposed to ratings for individual beers) based largely on the quality of the beer it brews, but also paying attention to other factors such as variety, style and efforts made to educate about beer.

The brewpubs listed below represent, we hope, an accurate listing of brewpubs as of 1992. However, because of the frequency with which brewpubs open and close, it can be difficult to maintain an up-to-date listing. Please feel free to inform us with brewpub information.

Prediction: Ontario will have more than fifty brewpubs by 1995.

TORONTO AREA

Amsterdam Brasserie & Brewpub
133 John Street, Toronto M4K 2E5

Brunswick Tavern
481 Bloor St. West, Toronto M5S 1X9

Denison's Brewing & Growler's Restaurant
204-2 Lombard Street, Toronto M5C 1M1

Granite Brewery (#2)
245 Eglinton Avenue East, Toronto M4P 3B7

Quinn's Tavern
940 Danforth Ave., Toronto M4J 1L9

Rotterdam Brewing Co.
600 King St. W., Toronto M5V 1M6

The Spruce Goose Brewing Co.
130 Eglinton Ave. E., Toronto M4P 2X9

CC's Brewpub
#1 6981 Mill Creek Drive, Mississauga L5N 6B8

Luxembourg Brewpub
4230 Sherwoodtowne Blvd,. Mississauga L4Z 2G6

Tapster's Brewhouse & Restaurant
100 Britannia Rd. E., Mississauga L4Z 2G1

Winchester Arms
255 Dundas St. W., Mississauga L5B 1J3

Marconi's Steak & Pasta House
262 Carlingview, Etobicoke M9W 5G1

Union Station Brewpub
4396 Steeles Ave. E., Markham L3R 9W1

Twist and Shout
9737 Yonge St., Richmond Hill L4C 8S7

Flying Dutchman Hotel & Lighthouse Brewpub
143 Duke St., Bowmanville L1C 2W4

Houston Track
60 Queen St. E., Brampton L6V 1A9

Luxembourg Brewpub No. 4
217 Cross Ave., Oakville L6J 2W9

Blue Anchor Brewery
47 West St., Orillia L3V 5G5

SOUTHWESTERN ONTARIO

Luxembourg Brewpub No. 2
1455 Lakeshore Rd., Burlington L7S 2J1

Suds International
1455 Lakeshore Rd., Burlington L7S 2J1

The Lion Brewery & Museum (Huether Hotel)
59 King Street North, Waterloo N2J 1S1

Heidelberg Restaurant & Brewery
2 King St., Heidelberg N0B 1Y0

The Queen's Inn
161 Ontario St., Stratford N5A 3H3

C.P.R. Tavern
671 Richmond St., London N6A 3G7

Mash McCann's
784 Dundas Street, London N5W 2Z7

Charley's Tavern
4715 Tecumseh Rd. E., Windsor N8T 1B6

EASTERN ONTARIO

Master's Brewpub
330 Queen Street, Ottawa K1R 5A5

Madawaska Tavern
59 Madawaska Street, Arnprior K7S 1S1

Kingston Brewing Co.
34 Clarence St,. Kingston K7L 1W9

NORTHERN ONTARIO

Jolly Friar Brasserie
320 Bay Street, Sault Ste. Marie P6A 1X1

Port Arthur Brasserie & Brewpub
901 Red River Rd., Thunder Bay P7B 1K3

6
POSTSCRIPT:
The Future of Beer
& How You Can Help
Shape It

What is the future of beer in Ontario? Despite the problems posed by a monopoly retail system, there will be some improvement for beerdrinkers in the 1990s. But problems will also persist.

Recent GATT-related trade decisions will eventually mean a somewhat better selection of imports. To compete in an increasingly competitive business, pubs will also offer a greater variety of quality beer. Brewpubs will continue to open at a dizzying rate; a few will close. Change in the brewery and microbrewery area will be slower.

The walls of protection and monopoly are crumbling quickly. We are beginning to see freer—if not free—trade in beer. But ironically, we believe that one of the main results of freer trade in beer will be that Ontario beerdrinkers will simply see a larger selection of Wet Air. More cheap product.

Because of the stranglehold that the LCBO-Brewers Retail monopoly holds on beer, it is unlikely that Ontarians will soon see the same choice of quality beer that Americans and Europeans enjoy. Even with Canada's fair trade obligations under GATT. The LCBO has little interest or expertise in beer, and will likely continue to demonstrate its belief that twenty or thirty types of beer is all its captive market deserves. Poor storage of beer and lack of knowledgeable service will also likely persist at the LCBO.

Freer trade in beer will have implications for brewers. We see little threat to small Ontario brewers who concentrate on quality. Many beerdrinkers argue that good beer, especially low-gravity beer, was never meant to travel long distances, and was certainly not meant to be stored for long periods of time. Quality brewing is, from this perspective, a local activity with local markets. This means that small brewers can only focus on quality and variety, know their market, and serve this market well.

Indeed, we believe that small brewers need to continue to improve their marketing. Marketing will have to be quite different from that of the large brewers. If the big brewers' goal is to take the water to the horse and whip and yell at her until she drinks (advertising), then the quality brewers' goal must be to lead the horse to water and encourage her to drink. Quality brewers must continually educate people about beer. The more beerdrinkers know about beer, the more they will seek out the best. Small brewers will have to demand a more educated staff at Brewers Retail. We would like to see more small brewers forge beer and cuisine links with chefs and restaurateurs. Finally, we expect to see more beer styles introduced by the small brewers.

For the larger brewers we see a variety of challenges posed by freer trade. We expect to see Molson's and Labatt's control of the "Beer Store" to be challenged by foreign brewers. "Minimum pricing" policies for beer will also be challenged. The "new brands listing fee" at Brewers Retail will likely have to be scrapped. Anti-competitive packaging regulations will be challenged, although progress toward ecologically effective packaging must be made. Stricter laws to prevent brewers from monopolizing or dominating the beer trade in pubs and licensed rooms may have to be enacted. Mandatory ingredients listing will be a reality within a decade.

We will be interested to see how the big Canadian brewers react to the coming wave of cheap, adjunct-laden suds from the U.S., and the pressure that the resulting decrease in marketshare will place on profits. As we see it, the wisest long-term strategy for Molson and Labatt to deal with this competition at the low end of the market is to ignore it. Molson and Labatt need to aim at the mid-market. They can do this by scrapping or improving their worst beers, by reversing the trend toward greater adjunct use, and by making their advertisements more intelligent, more focused on style, ingredients and brewing method. If they do things, the two large brewers will once again be seen by American and Canadian beerdrinkers as better, more quality-oriented brewers than the large Wet Air makers of the U.S.

How you can help: the Beer Ballot

The author of this book believes that one way to ensure that quality and variety continue to develop in the beers of Ontario is to involve drinkers themselves in giving feedback to brewers. Until now, we have not had much thoughtful public discussion of beer and brewing. Part of the reason for this is that we have lacked the forums needed for public discussion of beer as a quality beverage. Without these forums, improvement is difficult. Ontario has no public beer awards. Beer festivals are rare. Beer journalism and beer conversation are not a large part of the public discourse in this province, despite its beery roots.

To improve this situation, *The Ontario Beer Guide* invites you to send us your personal ratings of beer in several categories. We invite you to cast a vote for the beers you think superior in quality, given the demands of the style, with the "Beer Ballot" which follows this chapter.

Because (at present) beer in Ontario is overwhelmingly in just a few style categories, what might be separate categories in Europe or America have here been conflated. Pale ale and bitter, for example, have been conflated under "ale." Ales, even "pale ales" need not be pale, i.e., straw-coloured. The "strong beer" category does not distinguish between strong ales and strong lagers. Ditto "low-alcohol beer."

These fairly broad categories are unavoidable given the

character of the present provincial beer scene. If the categories were any narrower, we would have categories with only one example brewed. Therefore seven categories have been listed:

- Ale (pale ale or bitter)
- Stout
- Strong beer
- Low-alcohol beer
- Lager
- Bock
- Specialty beer

The bock category has the fewest examples at present (sadly), but may have more soon (we hope). "Specialty beer" covers wheat beer, eisbock, porter, and any other beer style not covered in the other six categories. You can vote for some or all of the categories; you needn't fill in every line of the Ballot. In addition, you can vote for best overall breweries, best brewpubs, and best pubs or bars for beer.

The next edition of *The Ontario Beer Guide* may require more categories. Please feel free to make suggestions for improving the Beer Ballot.

To cast a ballot in this poll, carefully detach (do not photocopy; only original ballots will be tabulated) the Beer Ballot, fill it in, and mail it to the address printed on the back of the ballot.

Results will be published in the next edition of *The Ontario Beer Guide*. Factors to consider when you vote include:

for **beer:**

- quality
- relationship to style

for **brewers:**

- quality and consistency of beer
- attention to beer style and/or successful stylistic innovation
- efforts made to educate about style and ingredients

for **brewpubs:**
- quality and consistency of a given beer
- variety of styles brewed
- efforts made to educate clients about beer
- ambience, including service, decor, and food

for **pubs & bars:**
- variety of beer sold, both on tap and in bottles
- draught situation: the care with which draught beer is kept and served; the fastidiousness with which the beer lines are maintained
- ambience, including service, decor and food

THE BEER BALLOT

Please vote only for *beers brewed in Ontario.*

Best Beers

Best ale (pale ale or bitter): _____

2nd-best ale: _____

3rd-best ale: _____

Best stout: _____

Best strong beer (6% alc./vol. or more): _____

Best low-alcohol beer (2.5-4% alc./vol.): _____

Best lager: _____

2nd-best lager: _____

3rd-best lager: _____

Best bock: _____

Best specialty beer: _____

2nd-best specialty beer: _____

Brewers of Ontario

Best brewery, overall: _____

Second-best brewery, overall: _____

Brewpubs of Ontario

Best brewpub overall: _____

2nd-best brewpub: _____

3rd-best brewpub: _____

Best brewpub ale: _____

Best brewpub lager: _____

Best brewpub specialty beer: _____

Best Pubs & Bars (not brewpubs) in Ontario

Best pub or bar for beer: _____

2nd-best pub or bar for beer: _____

Suggestions for improving the next Beer Ballot

_____

_____

_____

_____

_____

_____

_____

_____

_____

_____

_____

_____

_____

_____

Detach (do *not* photocopy) and mail to:
Beer Ballot
Riverwood Publishers Ltd.
P.O. Box 70, Sharon, Ontario L0G 1V0

Appendix A: Rating/Evaluation Sheet

[please photocopy]

Name
_____

Style _____ Pasteurized? _____ Filtered? _____

Tried with (other beers tried at same time) _____
_____

Auditory _____

Appearance (colour, head, lace) _____
_____

Aroma [4] _____
_____

Taste [10] (start, middle, finish) _____
_____
_____

Enjoyment [6] (including balance, plus auditory and appearance qualities) __
_____
_____

Other comments _____
_____

APPENDIX B
GLOSSARY OF BEER
AND BREWING
TERMINOLOGY

Note: Beer styles, ingredients and flavour words are described and defined in Chapter 3, "Understanding and Appreciating Beer."

Adjunct: any fermentable grain or sugar used to replace barley malt. In Canada, corn, especially corn syrup, is a common adjunct.

Amber: not a true style term. Denotes colour only. Often refers to ales.

Bitterness: one of the key flavours in many ales and lagers. Bitterness is detected at the back of the tongue.

Bitterness Units: International Bitterness Units (IBUs), are a conventional measure of the degree of bitterness in a beer. The threshold of detectability is 10-12 IBUs. Many mainstream beers have lost their bitterness over the years, and now are little more bitter than this threshold level. A moderately bitter Ontario pale ale or lager might have 20- 32 IBUs. Very bitter beers, i.e., porters and stouts, can have more than 50 IBUs.

Dry: in its traditional sense, dry simply means an "absence of sweetness." The term "dry" has, in the past decade, been attached to highly attenuated, low-flavour beers. The Japanese pioneered the use of genetically engineered yeast to ferment beer more fully. Much beer flavour, however, comes from unfermented matter. Pushing yeast to ferment malt sugars past their normal limits (high "attenuation") therefore results in more ethyl alcohol and less flavour, especially in the aftertaste, or finish.

Head: the foam on a glass of beer.

IBUs: see Bitterness Units.

Lace, lacing: sometimes called "Belgian lace," lace is the intricate and attractive remnants of the head which cling to the glass after the beer is drunk. A useful term, and often a good indicator of technical quality in a beer, especially of the quantity of malted barley used. Beers which leave no lace at all may have little malt in them. Look carefully at the lace in your empty glass: it can be beautiful.

Krausening: a form of late secondary fermentation with the aim of producing a soft and gentle carbonation, of augmenting "smoothness" without diminishing flavour. Unfermented malt sugars are added late in the fermentation, usually to the conditioning tank, and then slowly fermented out.

Malting: the process of turning raw barley grain into a ready-to-ferment food. It involves soaking the grains in water, allowing germination, and then stopping the germination at a precise point by drying and then (usually) roasting the grains. The longer the roast, or the higher the temperature, the darker the malt.

Original gravity ("O.G."): the density of the wort (see definition below) relative to water (which has a gravity of 1.000) before the yeast is pitched. An original gravity of 1048 means that the wort is 4.8% denser than water. High original gravity means that the wort has a relatively high level of malt sugars (partly) able to be converted to alcohol. The higher the original gravity, the higher the level of resulting alcohol, and/or the greater amount of unfermented matter (the source of much of beer's flavour) in the finished beer. In Ontario, an O.G. of more than 1050 would be considered high; an O.G. of less than 1042 would be considered low. When the yeast has done all its work converting fermentable sugars to alcohol, a final gravity ("F.G.") reading can be taken. This is apt to be 1005-1012. The difference between original and final gravity indicates the alcohol level.

Pasteurization: the killing of bacteria through heat. Pasteurization diminishes flavour because it also kills the beer. (Beer is "living" until it has been pasteurized or had all yeast removed. Beers with a yeast sediment in the bottom of the bottle are living beers: the yeast can be reused to ferment another batch of beer!)

Pitching: the addition of yeast to wort.

Real ale: an ale, usually made only with Reinheitsgebot ingredients, that is "naturally conditioned," i.e., naturally carbonated through gradual secondary or tertiary fermentation in the cask.

Reinheitsgebot: the German (Bavarian) beer purity law dating from 1516. The law stipulates that only barley malt, hops, and water may be used in the making of beer, with the use of yeast implied. In essence, the law means that no additives, chemicals, adjuncts (other than wheat, permitted under an amendment to the law) or preservatives (other than hops) are used. It also means that pasteurization (which kills flavour, as well as bacteria) is verboten. Few, if any, of the heavily advertised, mainstream North American beer brands meet the simple but rigid demands of this law.

Wort (pronounced "wert"): "pre-beer." The sweet malty liquid from which beer is made. Wort is about 95% water. Yeast is pitched into the wort to convert sugars into alcohol, and the wort is transformed into beer.

Zymurgy: the science and the art of fermentation.

Works Consulted & Further Reading

Books

Bowering, Ian. *In Search of the Perfect Brew*. General Store Publishing House, Burnstown, Ontario, 1990.

Bowering, Ian. *The Art and Mystery of Brewing in Ontario*. General Store Publishing House, Burnstown, Ontario, 1988.

Butcher, Alan D. *Ale and Beer: A Curious History*. McClellan and Stewart, Toronto, 1989.

Eckhardt, Fred. *The Essentials of Beer Style: A Catalog of Classic Beer Styles for Brewers and Beer Enthusiasts*. Fred Eckhardt Associates, Portland, Oregon, 1989.

Jackson, Michael. *Pocket Guide to Beer*. Simon and Schuster, New York, 1991.

Jackson, Michael. *The New World Guide to Beer*. Running Press, Philadelphia, 1988.

Papazian, Charlie. *The New Complete Joy of Homebrewing*. Avon Books, New York, 1991.

Magazines & Newsletters

All About Beer. Published by Bosak Publishing, Oceanside, California.

The Beer Bulletin. Published by CAMRA Ottawa.

What's Brewing. Published by CAMRA Canada.

What's Brewing. Published by CAMRA (U.K.).

Zymurgy. Published by the American Homebrewers Association.